IN THE COMPANY OF WOLVES

Anathema

IN THE COMPANY OF WOLVES

Anathema

STEVE LANG

For Dad

ACKNOWLEDGMENTS

Thanks to my family for always being there, no matter how difficult the road becomes.

TABLE OF CONTENTS

CHAPTER 1

THE COSMIC PORTAL CLOSED, AND Mac and his children were home again, standing with his new extended family on the shore of North Myrtle Beach, South Carolina. The late afternoon summer sun hung low in the sky, staring down at the Earth like a giant orange eye slowly closing, and night would soon be upon them. Waves tumbled over the shoreline as the tide rolled in, depositing hundreds of burrowing sand fleas. Mac watched little holes appear as if created by ghostly tunnel diggers and vanish with each recession of ocean water. Mac took a deep breath of the familiar salty sea air and listened to the seabirds squawking.

It almost felt like his childhood vacation home, but for the hotels lodged like lawn darts half a mile out in the ocean. Their destroyed frames were evidence that some unknown calamity had befallen Earth.

"Nice place you have here, Mac," Dante said. "Daddy, what happened to the beach?" Serena asked.

She was thirteen now and had grown a full inch taller. Mac could see more of Carol's features on her face, which were hazy but reminiscent, like a mirage. One minute she looked like his little girl and another, it was as if she were the perfect likeness to Carol. Bobby looked older, too, with a complete five o'clock shadow covering the lower half of his face, foreshadowing the man he would soon become.

"My guess is a tsunami hit this beach, probably just after we escaped," Mac said.

An entire forest had grown where there was once a thriving tourist industry.

"Do you know where we are?" Lilith asked.

"I believe we're on Myrtle Beach. It's the last thing I thought about before opening the cosmic portal. "But I don't know what year it is," Mac said.

"Well, the sun's going down. Should we camp here for the night?" Ramos asked.

"Sleeping on the beach is not bad, plus we can probably fish the surf for dinner," Mac said.

"This is the first time Serena, and I have ever been to the beach, Dad," Bobby said. The teen surveyed the damaged buildings decaying in the ocean and sighed.

"Sorry it couldn't have been under better circumstances, kids," Mac said.

"We need to eat, and I'm a fairly good angler. I'll fly up and see if anything is swimming close to the shoreline," Lilith said.

In the fading afternoon sun, she looked like a vision of pure beauty to Mac, and he thought the kids also seemed to like her.

"I know I don't need to tell you this, but be careful out there," Mac said.

"What is this careful you speak of? Alright, be back soon," Lilith said. She smiled at the children, and in an instant, the whoosh of her wings fanned Bobby and Serena.

"Can you please see what else you can find up there, Lilith? Buildings inland that are intact, anywhere we might shack up for a night," Mac said. She nodded back at him and flew away. Ramos was testing his magic as he conjured a purple fireball and tossed it into the air. It rose and arced like a flare, falling into the sand about fifty yards from them.

"That's so cool! Can you teach me how to do it?" Bobby said.

"I'm afraid not, Bobby," Ramos said. He remembered when his spirit left his body in the cave, the purple orb invading his mind, and his encounter with Inga.

"It just seems like you guys and my dad get to have all the fun, and I want to join in," Bobby said.

"It's a strange Universe, my young friend. Who knows what the future holds for you?" Ramos said.

Bobby ran over to where the purple ball landed and watched it cool—as acrid smoke wafted to his nostrils—turning the sand, it melted into a solid orb of purple glass. Bobby touched it and felt electricity surge as he flew several feet onto his back. What he did not know was that deep within the cortex of his brain, a new neural pathway opened.

"Bobby! Are you alright?" Mac said.

Bobby lay still on the sand, listening as roaring waves washed over the beach for a moment longer. Microscopic tendrils of supernatural energy sprouted like new vines, enhancing his synaptic strength as he sat up and shook his head.

"That was intense," Bobby grunted. He stood and walked over to the ball, which was now clear and cool.

"What happened to him?" Mac asked.

"I'm not sure, but the orb was discharged when Bobby touched it. How do you feel?" Ramos asked. "OK, I guess. I touched Ramos's ball, and then next thing I knew, I was staring up at the sky," Bobby said.

"Jeez, well, try to be more careful," Mac said. "Yeah, dad," Bobby replied.

Ramos stood facing the ocean and shaking his head, then turned toward the dense forest cover.

"What lives in that water and these woods? Is it safe to camp here?

"I have no idea anymore, but if there are still people around maybe they can give us some information or shelter," Mac said.

Lilith soared into the air and looked down upon the water as she searched for their dinner. While she hunted, Lilith saw jellyfish the size of small cars, schools of eight-foot-long fish, and sea turtles larger than a little house. From her peripheral vision, she caught the shadow of a giant whale, two hundred feet long, submerged just below the water's surface, with long tentacles flowing out from behind.

Curiosity got the better of her, and she drifted toward the whale for a closer look. Instinct and her peripheral vision set her on alert, and Lilith rolled to the side before being eaten as the behemoth leaped from the water, its mouth agape like the opening of a giant dark cave. Instinctively, she flipped backward and threw two blazing fireballs into the creature's mouth.

The monster gave a grunting screech as flames exploded inside its throat, cooking it from within. Lilith was a mile from shore and cut off from her party as the beast fell to the sea, a tentacle wrapped around her foot, dragging her toward the black depths below. Lilith slammed into the salty ocean and was dragged into the frozen depths as the dead whalestrosity sank like a boulder. She calmed her panic and reached down to dislodge her ankle from the tentacle, which had sucker cups on the bottom with barbs, and the more she tried to unwrap it, the more deeply dug in they became.

Her lungs burned for oxygen, and she felt the pressure of the ocean crushing her body. Tugging, pushing, and clawing at the tentacle was useless as she started to lose hope. A sizeable, fast-moving shape came toward her: the shadow of a monster twice the size of the one dragging her down. As it neared, she saw nothing but a wall of teeth, each one easily larger than the length of her body. The mouth opened, and as she shut her eyes, preparing for the end, it closed on the whale; the much larger shark bit down on the whale monster, severing the tentacle, allowing her to break free and swim for the surface. Only about a foot was wrapped around her leg when she looked down.

Lilith exploded out of the salty water, its weight weighing her wings down like a boat anchor. But Lilith could fly, and with some effort, she made it to one skeletal hotel with a metal frame sign above it reads *Callaway Resort*; the glass had long ago been blown out, and now the rusted frame clung to the derelict building on aging bolts, creaking in the wind. She landed on the roof and knelt to unwrap the remaining tentacle from her leg, giving an involuntary shudder as she tossed it back into the ocean.

After the traumatic experience, Lilith needed some time to rest, so she lay down on the roof, her wings acting as a bed beneath her. When her eyes closed, an underwater dream world movie presented her with a massive shark mouth, deadly teeth, and a horrifying creature attached to it. Lilith opened them again two hours later and sat up, still feeling the exhilaration of fresh evening air wisp about her wings and body. She thought about her past.

She pressed the heels of her palms against her closed eyes and felt some of the pressure behind their release.

"Welcome home," Lilith said.

As night descended, she watched the flickering campfire light on the darkened beach and could smell the aroma of fish cooking. She sat longer, listening to the waves lap against the hotel in an almost hypnotic, rhythmic shoosh for a bit longer. Then Lilith stepped to the edge of the building and felt it vibrate beneath her feet. She flexed her wings to prepare to take flight, but the curiosity below captured her attention. The building vibrated again, this time almost knocking her over.

"Earthquake?" Lilith whispered, and then she saw the source.

Gliding around the hotel was the enormous shark that had saved her life earlier that day, and as it passed, a brilliant moonlight glimmered off its rigid gray body. It would have been easy if the building were tall. The shark was more massive than any she had seen, and its dorsal fin was half the height of her perch. The shark circled her building three times, turning to the side with a slight roll. The large black eye stared at her like an onyx orb, a window into the abyss. The ferocity in those eyes gave her a chill, and for a moment, she wondered how far this thing could leap out of the water.

"You're hunting me," Lilith said. "Naughty, naughty," she said with a smile.

The shark was too giant and close to attack directly, and she wanted to avoid killing the beast that saved her life if she could. As it passed her once more, rounding the horseshoe-shaped hotel, Lilith shot straight into the air and flew hundreds of feet above the water. The shark had never seen her go and continued his lazy circle around and around as Lilith got away.

A few minutes later, she walked toward Mac on dry land. He and the others had been huddled around the campfire, and all else was dark outside their ring. When her feet touched down, they were as soft as an angel's whisper, and the wolven never heard her coming. Mac was standing next to a tree, staring into the starlit sky, when she placed her hand on his shoulder. He jumped under her touch, and she could feel him tense.

"Crap!" Mac said. "Nervous?" Lilith laughed.

"Haha, good one. What happened to you?" Mac asked. He turned and wrapped his arms around her, which, in human form, put his face right at breast height.

"Whale trouble, and you would not believe the size of the shark I escaped from. It was easily the size of a building," Lilith said.

"Are you sure this is your planet? Can we enter another realm or dimension that looks like your Earth?" Ramos asked.

"I have no idea. Before we left, there was nothing like what Lilith described in the water anywhere in the world. There were stories we'd hear of large sharks called megalodon, and divers would even find their teeth scuba diving, so maybe that's what it was," Mac said.

"Have a seat and eat some fish, Lilith. It's good," Bobby said. His hands were full of a large chunk of cooked fish, and he was taking another bite. "Yeah, Dante attacked a school swimming too close to shore. You should have seen him carrying on out there. It was all teeth and claws slapping at the water. I'm amazed he caught anything," Ramos said.

"Don't criticize my tactics and sit there eating my catch, Ramos," Dante barked.

"Well, that's one way to do it. I could have saved myself some trouble and stayed here," Lilith said. "A lot's changed since we left. It's scary, really," Mac said.

"Yeah, and we haven't even been beyond the beach yet," Serena said.

"Well, no permanent damage done," Lilith said. She unconsciously rubbed the red spots on her leg where the tentacles had attached to her. They were swollen and filled with a greenish puss.

"What's wrong with your leg?" Ramos said.

"A side effect of my encounter with that whale," Lilith replied.

"Something like that could kill you if the infection spreads," Mac said.

"Sweetie, I've had way worse," Lilith smiled.

"I think it's a good idea to stick together from here on, just until we get a better idea of what we're dealing with here," Mac said.

"You know, that's how the movie monsters get you. They separate the idiots and take them down one at a time until there's only one left," Bobby said.

"I saw a town beyond the trees," Lilith said. "That must be Ocean Drive. Let's look tomorrow; there may be some people there who can fill us in on A, what year this is, and B, what has been happening since we left," Mac said. "Good idea. See what else this place has to eat. The fish here are delicious," Dante said. He was holding a piece of fish the size of his head.

Lilith sat beside Bobby, ate for the first time since leaving Eritria, and gazed at Mac. He was still somewhat of a mystery but one she was growing fonder of each day. He had the demeanor of a gentleman but fought like a ferocious warrior. She had seen the feral rage in his eyes during the battle with the Cyclops and again when the reptilians charged through that cosmic portal.

One curiosity was the feral rage within him, and Mac's human side vanished as he clawed and chewed his way through the ranks of Asura's army.

"Lightning out on the sea," Dante said. He pointed a greasy finger to the dark horizon where long zig-zagging strikes were zapping the water in clusters. "Storm's coming."

"I'm not so sure it's a normal storm," Mac said. "Before the crap hit the fan here, there were freak atmospheric anomalies that caused lightning storms to erupt out of the blue. If that lightning stays over there, we should be OK,"

"You don't want to get caught in one," Bobby said.

"Mr. Potter, the drugstore owner in town, was hit by four lightning bolts one day. One after the other. I saw it happen," Serena said.

"Yeah, and remember when Ms. Gaston walked her dog, and the lightning got her? It struck her so hard that she was knocked out of her shoes and into the path of Doug Deegle's pickup truck. He didn't even have time to react and bump, bump under she went," Bobby said.

He spoke in a matter-of-fact tone as he ate. Mac was surprised to see how desensitized his children had become to violence and horror.

"Was this after I left for Eritria?" Mac asked. "Yeah. After you took off, things went downhill, but the worst was when Aunt Lorraine died," Bobby said.

Bobby said no more and picked a fish bone out of his teeth, flipping it over his shoulder and going onto the beach.

"We have all seen terrible things and survived to talk about it," Ramos said.

All nodded, and as the campfire illuminated their faces, Mac thought about how lucky he was to have such good friends with him in his upside-down home world.

As he watched the lightning flicker out at sea, Mac was grateful to be with his family, human once more.

"I don't know about the rest of you, but I feel like I haven't slept in three weeks," Mac said.

"We should all stay close tonight," Ramos said. "We don't know what night predators walk these lands," Dante said.

"I agree," Lilith said. She closed her eyes, saw the whale's jaws, and quickly opened them again.

"You'll be safe with us, Lilith. I'm using my last protection spell, so we'll all sleep safely. Not even that lightning can penetrate the power of this field," Ramos said.

As he lay down, Mac reminisced about his younger years, and sunny days, running up and down the beach, playing in the sand without a care. His mother and father were there then, watching him gallivant in and out of the surf.

He drifted off to sleep a few minutes later and dreamed of a bleak world and a gray, colorless forest, where the trees were devoid of leaves and a thick mist gathered around his feet. A dense fog moved with him, blocking his visibility of what lay beyond as he took one careful step after another. Something long and black slithered by his foot, and as he looked down, he saw his white feet sinking into the thick muck. Mac was in human form and confused, sensing darkness ahead. He walked forward and saw the mist part before him, and a gate appeared in the clearing.

It was a wrought iron fence crafted with decorative swirling patterns, making the gate appear tangled with thorny black vines. It creaked open, and Mac walked toward it like a man trapped on a moving sidewalk, as a voice whispered in his head.

"You will never find peace," The voice said.

Mac saw images of sorrow and a bleak future in the afterworld. He saw himself crucified on a telephone pole, his wolven form decaying in the gloom, the white fur now sullied with grime and blood.

"There is no absolution, only the dry sorrow of your everlasting soul. You will walk the world in obscurity for all time," The voices said.

Mac could picture himself walking through a barren land, completely alone. Dropping to his knees, he began to cry as the faces of the thousand nameless victims from the underground lab faded in and out of the fog. They were the accusers, condemning him for his part in their demise. Mac felt his heart squeeze, his chest tightened, and he fell to his knees, digging his fingers into the muck.

"No!" Mac said.

Mac looked up to see the tornado of souls, the spirits of his nameless jury of the dead spinning about him, like the jury at his last trial.

"We are COMING!" The voices said, screaming now in unison.

Mac sat straight up, his leg kicking the cosmic portal beside him on the beach.

Sweating and still reeling from the immense sorrow in his nightmare, Mac sat up and watched the tide roll in. The tide was further out now, which extended the beach by about a hundred feet, and in the distance, Mac could see two enormous ghost crabs battling one another by the water. They must have been three feet tall, he thought. He changed back to wolven form, feeling increasingly more secure with teeth and claws than with his pulse rifle. Lilith's bow was beside her in the sand, and so was Dante's. Ramos's sword was still neatly tucked away inside his robe, and he wondered for a moment what it would be like to wield it for even a moment.

"What happened here?" Mac whispered.

A figure moved to his right, and as Mac turned, cold fear rose from the base of his spine, tingling the tips of the hair on his ears. Obscured by darkness, a five-foot-tall grey man stood about ten feet from him. Mac stood up and faced the strange figure before him.

Illumination from behind by his craft, Mac could see a man in a grey skintight suit staring at him with unblinking almond-shaped black eyes. His nose was a horizontal slit on his face, followed by a sideways reddish-brown insectoid mandible, like a pinching bug. As the man stared at Mac, his jaws clicked open and closed twice, making a sharp clicking sound. Icy fingers clawed Mac's back as his mind went blank with fear.

"The egg, give it to me," A voice inside his head said in a slow hiss.

The man had thin, spindly fingers at the end of his long, skinny arms. Mac felt an excruciating pain in his head after this demand, as if a truck horn were blaring in his ears.

"Give me the egg by your feet, or you all die," The voice said again.

Next came the sound of a million locusts, punishing his mind and amplifying to jet engine volume. A trickle of blood ran down Mac's nose and another out of his ear.

"OK!" Mac screamed.

Mac knelt, his hands pressing against his ears, to pick up the case as Dante lifted his head, blinking slowly. Ramos awoke next. The two wolven brothers soon realized they could move no further than raising their heads.

"Please, make it stop!" Mac screamed. Tears of agony streamed down his cheeks.

He could not grab the case, so he kicked it across to the alien, who had begun sending wave after wave of nausea-inducing sound waves into his mind. After the case was by the man's feet, the sirens in Mac's head stopped, and he dropped to the ground in the fetal position. Mac felt incapacitated as he watched the cosmic portal levitate above the ground by unseen hands. The alien removed an instrument that resembled a tuning fork from the pouch around his waist and taped it to the side of the solid metal box.

The metal shell began to crack like an egg, and the box split in two in a few more seconds. What spilled out was a creature about the size of a tennis ball but shaped like an aphid. The man in the suit took another instrument out of his pocket and clicked a button. A laser light hit the aphid creature, and it grew and transformed into a smaller three-foot version of the man holding the laser. When it completed the transformation, what stood before them was a duplicate of the other, taller man.

"You stole my child, Earthman!" The voice said again.

It was enraged, and suddenly Mac felt the indescribable pain in his head again; this time, the volume had been turned up even louder. He felt as if the entire world were splitting in two, and as he writhed on the ground, he began to wish the alien would kill him.

When he thought he could take no more, the noise stopped, and everything went silent. Mac looked up to see the smaller child put her hand on the enraged insectoid man's hand and saw her shake her head. She pointed to Mac, lying on the ground, and then gave a strange salute to the adventurers. The taller alien nodded. Without another word, the two turned and walked toward the spacecraft. A moment later, a ramp descended from the darkness beyond, and the two stepped aboard.

The starship that had been the EBE, Klactu's home for over three hundred years, rose from the ground once more and disappeared into the stars. He had crossed six dimensions of time and space to find little Greng and hatch her from the lyrca egg. Now that he had his daughter back, he would sleep an entire night for the first time in many years.

"Crap!" Mac said. He was wiping the blood from his ears as he stood up.

"What?" Ramos asked. Everyone was awake and able to move.

"Stephanie and Kim are still trapped on Eritria, and that cosmic portal, alien egg thing was our only way to get them back," Mac said.

They all looked to the stars with heavy hearts because Dante and Ramos realized they were trapped on Earth just as they were.

CHAPTER 2

THE SUN ROSE ON A brand-new day on the South Carolina coastline as Mac woke from a dreamless sleep. The humidity rose, and his skin felt clammy from the salty air. The alien's psychological assault left Mac mentally spent, and his head was pounding as if he'd been on a cheap whiskey bender, but he still took inventory of the team.

Dante was relieving himself in a bush about twenty feet from the campsite, and Ramos sat in quiet contemplation, facing the ocean. Bobby sat up and began to eat a half-charcoaled hunk of leftover fish, and in another moment, Serena joined him. She sat beside her brother, wiping the sleep from her eyes, and looked serene as she watched a flock of seagulls pass over the ocean just offshore. Lilith was gone.

"So, how'd everyone sleep?" Bobby asked.

"Not very well, unfortunately. I remember a disturbance in the night," Ramos said.

"Yeah, I passed out sometime after my ears stopped bleeding. Do you kids remember anything from last night?" Mac asked.

"I dreamed about Mom again," Serena said. "Yeah, me too," Bobby said.

"It is still strange not having her with us. So, what was your dream about?" Mac said. "Well, I was in this fog, and then after I walked through it, there was an open gate," Bobby said. Mac's mind returned to the dark dream, thick pea soup mist, and his gate.

"Yeah, me too. I saw Mommy on the other side, and she was smiling at me. There were green trees and grass. She was holding flowers in her hands, and it felt like I could walk right through," Serena said.

"That's what happened to me! I ran to her, but she said if I tried to cross now, there would be darkness, and the green trees would die because it is not my time to cross," Bobby said.

Mac nodded and gave his children a wan smile. "Do you remember waking up and seeing anything last night?" Mac asked.

"Nope, slept all night. Why, what happened, Dad?" Bobby asked.

"Something came and took the cosmic portal, or hatched it, rather; I think it was an egg. This man with a pincher bug mouth that looked like one of those grey aliens," Mac said.

"It was one of the strangest experiences of my life," Ramos said. "And I've died once already,"

"I think the smaller alien that came out of the cosmic portal saved our lives," Mac said.

Dante walked over to the camp. "What's going on? What are we talking about?"

"The oddity last night," Mac said. "Oh, you mean us getting trapped on your planet. Yeah, I never want to talk about that. Where's tall, dark, and sexy?" Dante asked.

"I have no idea where she went, but Lilith was here last night when the weirdness went down," Mac said.

"Whatever it was, didn't get this!" Bobby said, pointing to the tablet.

"See, it could have been way worse," Mac said. The tablet lay on the sand by Bobby. The fifteen-year-old had been carrying a backpack filled with miscellaneous items from home that he thought would be useful in a life-and-death situation. He removed the pack, unzipped it, and placed the tablet inside.

"Looks like we found a real use for that pack, kid," Mac laughed.

As Mac zipped the pack deep inside Bobby's brain, the purple tendrils grew stronger and faster. For an instant, after Bobby put the pack back on Mac, he saw a purple spark in Bobby's eyes, and then it was gone.

Serena was cupping her hands over her eyes like a visor. "There she is! Lilith's sitting over on that broken-down hotel again."

The hotel was a mile away, and Lilith was sitting on the roof's edge, her legs dangling over the side. She drifted on a sea of memories and wondered if she should tell Mac this was not her first time on Earth. It seemed natural enough, but since leaving the planet thousands of years ago, she had never needed to explain her origins.

Long ago, in another age, the makers crafted her to serve as a concubine for the first genetically evolved man in this world. Lilith came to life in Ninhursag's laboratory as a manufactured wife for the human king of the slaves, Adamu. She remembered the sterile environment, the white- walled chamber where they educated her to serve the gods and held her against her will, and as she sat in the hotel, her mind drifted back thirty-five thousand years to the weeks after her creation.

Enki entered the room as Ninhursag completed the last of her genetic modifications. They Anunnaki were gods and giants to the people of Earth, standing ten feet five inches, with broad shoulders, and wearing their people's golden threaded, white linen robes. His features were those of modern-day humans with high cheekbones, oval eyes, and long blond hair. Enki walked with a powerful stride, an immortal, with muscular arms and legs. He ruled the people of Earth with an iron fist with the help of his brother Enlil. Ninhursag was the picture of beauty and grace, revered by the humans as the lady of the mountain, who worshiped her with beautifully crafted artwork, clay figurines, and jewelry.

Lilith remembered what Ninhursag had explained to her about their origins. The Anunnaki were from Nibiru and had come to Earth to mine the precious minerals in her soil. In their race to master technology, they had inadvertently destroyed their atmosphere, and the gold they mined was pulverized into a powder known as the philosopher's stone. This powdered gold was distributed into their beloved planet's atmosphere to deflect the sun's harmful rays and repair the damage done. Now in their hundred thousandth year of mining on Earth, the Anunnaki handled mining operations until they realized that the Neanderthal man was far better equipped to handle the heat of the mines and the strenuous toil of mining gold.

"Is she ready to go?" Enki asked.

"Almost. The serum I administered will grant the subject long-lasting life. Unlike some of our lesser creations, she will never need to replenish by eating the philosopher's stone," Ninhursag said.

"These humans have been a wonderful addition to the mining effort, but they can never know the secret to our immortality. Will she tell?" Enki said.

"Never. Is Adamu prepared to receive his bride?" Ninhursag asked. She was grinning at him, her mouth upturned in a wry smile.

"General Sang informed the human king that she will be joining him by the end of the week," Enki said.

Lilith sat on the edge of the laboratory table, her wings dark and shimmering. Black feathers that shone brightly under fluorescent lights, reflecting the light. Her skin was pale as a spring morning fog, and her face was archetypal. She was a blank slate for the Anunnaki and waited impatiently for the day she would join her mate on Earth. They told her that Adamu was a ruler among mere men, closest ally to the gods Anu, Enki, and Enlil, and would be a good mate for her.

"I am very excited to leave and see Earth," Lilith said. Her dark eyes sparkled with her newness to life, and she felt her pulse quicken at the thought of experiencing her life for the first time.

"That's good. Exceptionally good. Because you will tomorrow if this serum doesn't turn foul overnight, that is," Ninhursag said.

"Turn?" Enki asked.

"It's a bit experimental on this body type, but I have a mouse that's managed to survive one hundred years past its expiration date with the same formula," Ninhursag said.

"You don't plan on giving that to the other humans, do you? We tried long life in this race before, and in every case, it led to disobedience and lawlessness. Wars broke out in the mines and human leaders charged our sentries with armies. It was a nightmare, and each time, we had to put them down and start over with a new batch of workers.

"It will be fine, don't worry so much." It's just that this batch of workers fears us, understands our orders, and is less likely to disobey our commands, so can we please stop tinkering with them?" Enki said.

"I'm done tinkering with them, but Lilith is my finest hour, my most proud creation. I love her," Ninhursag said. She kissed Lilith on the mouth. "Don't start playing with the pets again," Enki scowled.

"What is a pet?" Lilith asked.

"A pet, my dear, is a beautiful, wonderful thing. My husband does not share my fascination with the creation of higher lifeforms," Ninhursag said.

"All I mean is that you keep getting too attached to your work," Enki said.

Ninhursag smiled at Lilith and ran the back of her hand from the smoothness of her cheek down to her naked arm and thigh.

"Does this please you?" Ninhursag asked Lilith. "Yes," Lilith said. Her heart was racing inside hey chest at the other woman's caress.

"Enki, do be a dear and close the door behind you. I want some time alone to perform some more...experiments on our lovely young lady here," "Alright, but if this all turns out badly and we havr to destroy your experiments again, I do not want to see one tear in your eye," Enki said.

He turned and left as the creator and creation spent the next few hours exploring each other's bodies, the landscape of love. Lilith learned more that day than she ever had, and she would soon find out that her first time with Adamu would be a pale comparison to the sexual joy Ninhursag had brought her in the few hours they shared.

The next morning, Lilith was taken from the confines of her stark white room and placed aboard one of the Vimana starships for transport to Terra. The V-shaped craft sat in the spaceport hanger and resembled a bird in flight.

"Lilith, are you nervous?" Ninhursag asked.

"A little. What's the world like?" Lilith asked. "Harsh, unforgiving, and beautiful, but you will reign over these people in time. The man you will couple with will age, wither, and die, but you will stay forever young, immortal," Ninhursag said. When Enki landed his ship by the palace of Adamu in what would eventually be the desert near modern- day Iraq, he extended the ramp, and all three of them walked out into the bright sunlight. Adamu stepped out of his home to greet them, but he was nothing like Lilith expected.

The man Lilith was to be wed to be a five-foot- tall stooping character with a thick brow, bushy eyebrows, and a sloping forehead. His hair was long and brown, unkempt, and he smelled like sweltering summer sweat and dirt. He had powerful arms and wore a maroon pallium. His initial demeanor was suspicious toward the winged woman, his new wife, and he looked to Enki for confirmation.

"Adamu, we present Lilith. She will be your wife, and the two of you shall procreate and fill the land with your descendants," Enki said.

Lilith gave the hulking man an unsure smile, and he returned it with a scowl.

"You are mine, now. Thank you, Enki. I will do as you say, and our children will multiply a bounty of workers for the gold mine," Adamu said.

"We'll leave you two alone to get acquainted," Enki said.

"Yes, and Lilith, remember that Adamu is your lord and master now and your husband," Ninhursag said. She gave Lilith a sad smile and winked at her before turning to go.

The first three weeks did not go well for Lilith; Adamu continually harassed her. He demanded sexual satisfaction but gave none in return. She felt like a sheep in the pen waiting for the next time when he would insert his male part into her, take what he wanted, and leave the room like a thief after finishing. Lilith began to resent Adamu until one night, she fled. Capturing a boat from one of the fishers, she sailed to an island where she could remain hidden for several weeks. However, Adamu had reported her missing to the Anunnaki, and they sent winged emissaries to find her. The men came with spears that projected fierce lightning bolts from the tip and tried to use them to scare her.

"We will return you to Adamu; it is preordained that you be together. You are coming with us, or we will drown you in the ocean," said a dark-winged man.

"You may as well kill me now if you can. I'm not going anywhere with you," Lilith said. She was intense and terrifying to behold.

They were unprepared for her ire and eventually fled, but not before cursing her name.

"You will forever be reviled as a demon sent to this world to steal the children of men. Your name will be forever known as a seducer, a thief of men's souls, and they will curse you as if you were the devil," said one of the angels.

Lilith bade them farewell and vanished until the great cataclysm of Nibiru forced her to evacuate the planet on an escaping starship. Living in seclusion on the isle of Crete, she was abandoned by the watchers and other Anunnaki priests, banished and shunned by her creators. Granted a second wife, Adamu named her Eve, and together they did procreate and lived as the creators commanded, but Adamu's descendants would experience one of the most terrifying events any human had ever seen when the home planet of the Anunnaki, Nibiru, made a pass by Earth. The giant planet looked like a small dot of light in the sky, another star that grew progressively brighter for years until she became a terrifying vision in the Earthling sky. Nibiru came so close on her procession through the stars that she almost touched the planet Earth, causing worldwide tsunamis that nearly obliterated all life on the small blue planet. Had Enlil not warned the people of Earth that their world was about to be destroyed, a boat containing the genetic code of every living animal on Earth could not have been constructed in time, and all life would have perished in the tumult. Lilith knew of the coming trouble and stowed away on a science ship bound for the Zeta Reticuli star system to hide the Tablets of Destinies. Secreted away for thousands of years on Earth inside the temple of Olympus, the Anunnaki realized they would have to move them when the celestiae collision with Nibiru became imminent.

The tablets expertly scribed inscriptions, rumored to contain the power of the universe, almost vibrated with energy. In distant ages, entire planets fell to their destructive power, like wheat fields under the farmer's scythe because of misuse. When Commander Arduk discovered Lilith hiding in one of the cargo bays, he spared her life.

"You know, we could eject you out into space for stowing away aboard this ship," Arduk said. "Please, I needed to get off Earth, and I can help you when you arrive on Eritria if you let me," Lilith said.

The commander considered her for a moment. "Alright, let's see what you can do. We need all the help we can get,"

When Lilith arrived on Eritria, she was assigned to modify Eritria's animals genetically. The program's purpose was to evolve the creatures of the planet, much as they had on Earth, only this time wolves, bears, reptiles, moles, bulls, and many other animals would serve as subjects for the tinkering of a privileged, ancient race of people from the stars. Her story about having parents on Eritria had been a rouse. They were Egren, of course, but Lilith was the first of their kind and creator, and they were her protectors sworn to secrecy about her identity.

During her schooling as a gene manipulator, she created a race of people from her own body. She could keep her activities covert for a time, but he was furious when Arduk discovered she was keeping her race secret. Arduk confronted her in the laboratory one evening.

"You have violated the laws of creation, Lilith! Our mission is to evolve the existing races, not act as the one true God does!" Arduk said.

"I never meant to violate anything, Arduk," Lilith said. "You and your subjects shall be banished from here to the land of Valuria, deep within this planet," Arduk said.

"What's my alternative?" Lilith asked. Her eyes were pleading.

"The immediate execution of you and every one of your abominations," Arduk said.

"How is what you do different from what I've done?" Lilith asked.

"We act as emissaries across the multidimensional framework of time to speed up progress where it is deemed necessary and good for the beings of the planet. It takes time, years sometimes, to examine the life forms, their environment, and the feasibility of such an undertaking. You selfishly created a new race of people that may not comply with the current geo- forming of our designs for this planet," Arduk said.

"Turned away again? I see how it is. You're all the same," Lilith said.

She picked up a surgical knife from a table next to her and jammed it into Arduk's neck. The commander grasped the handle of the blade and removed it from his throat, but when he did, a tidal wave of blood gushed out, and the ten-foot-tall man fell to his face on the unyielding steel floor. He was gasping like a fish out of water as his mouth worked open and closed, and then he died. Lilith, now hunted by the Anunnaki forever, vanished with her people to the underworld of Valuria. She was never seen again as life flourished above their heads in the daylight of Eritria.

Something splashed below her in the dark ocean water. Lilith looked down and noticed that her friend, the massive shark, was back and circling the building again.

"You again?"

The shark dived under, disappearing beneath the black tide.

"Uh-oh. Where'd you go?" Lilith said. She stood and walked the perimeter of the building, looking for the monster for five minutes.

In another few seconds, she saw it again; the twenty-five-foot fin rising above the water was all she saw as it sped toward her like a torpedo. Lilith shot into the air just in time to miss becoming lunch for the shark as it launched one hundred feet in a massive arc over the building.

"What the...?!" Lilith said.

Its tail struck the Avista Resort sign, knocking it into the water, and it sank to the bottom of the sea like an anchor. Lilith flew toward shore as the hungry shark reared out of the water, a towering goliath of sinewy muscle, the world's oldest predator, alive with ferocity not seen by many human eyes on those bleak days. She touched down on the beach as the shark made another pass, slamming into the building, knocking it over and into the ocean on its back. Her perch sank into the water as ancient vacation rooms filled with water, and in minutes, the derelict hotel vanished from sight forever.

"That was a great vacation spot," Mac said. He was shaking his head as the grand old haunt of his youth sank below the waves.

"I'm fine, by the way," Lilith said.

" I was concerned for your welfare, but if you had seen that place when it was new," Mac said.

"I, for one, would not mind getting as far away from this beach as possible before that shark realizes you're up here and decides to try out his land legs," Dante said.

"That's fine with me. Let's go," Lilith said. "What were you doing out there? "No, wait, nonl of my business," Mac said.

"I was just going over some old memories, spending some time alone," Lilith said and hugged Mac around his neck. I love you," she whispered. I love you, too," Mac said, kissing her.

"Daddy, are we going into the woods?" Serena asked.

"I don't see any other choice," Mac said. He looked up and down at the beach. A substantial wall of trees and bushes was blocking their way, as if the forest were trying to protect itself from the ocean.

"OK, so how do we get through? Those trees are thick," Bobby said. "I could blast through there with a few balls of fire," Lilith replied.

"Just out of curiosity, how far away is Egypt?" Ramos asked.

"The other side of the world," Mac said. "And the cosmic portal could take you anywhere you concentrated your mental energy?" Dante asked.

"So why are we on Myrtle Beach instead of Egypt?" Ramos asked.

"Because I have never been there and don't know exactly where we would have ended up. I had a vivid image of this place, so that's why we're here. Next time, we'll put it to a vote, OK?" Mac retorted.

"Boys don't fight. We have work to do." Lilith said.

They all stood facing the thick bushes and densely packed-together trees.

"So, how do we get through?" Bobby asked. Ramos's eyes went full and bright. "We can use this!" Ramos said. He pulled out his sword hilt and gripped it, smiling as a blade of flames ushered forth.

"Can I use it?" Bobby asked.

Ramos turned toward Mac for approval.

"Sure, why not? Just don't burn the place down," Mac said.

Ramos deactivated the sword and handed the hilt to Bobby. A few tense seconds passed as the boy gripped it in his two hands, trying to figure out how to turn it on, and just as Ramos was about to speak, the sword came alive.

"Got it!" Bobby said.

They watched in amusement as he sliced through his first tree, and then another until a visible path formed. The odor of burning wood and the crack of falling timber broke the silence of an overcast morning.

"This is awesome!" Bobby said. "Thanks, Ramos."

"Don't mention it, just don't miss and accidentally hit one of us," Ramos said.

"You got it," Bobby said.

As Bobby continued to hack and slash his way through the forest, Mac thought he could see the remnants of Ocean Drive somewhere through the gloom and wondered why he had opened the portal on Myrtle Beach. Ramos and Dante were right; it made no sense to prolong their journey, and he felt that this would be the first of many long days back on planet Earth.

CHAPTER 3

BOBBY HACKED AND SLASHED FROM the beach to the town ruins in about twenty minutes as the rest of his party followed him, watching the woods for strange animals and dangers unseen. Bobby stepped from the forest onto Ocean Drive for the first time, astonished at how much it resembled one of those ancient ruins he had seen on the Discovery Channel documentaries.

He could make out what used to be a road running through town, the asphalt, long ago ripped apart. Tall trees grew through the cinder block skeletons of old buildings. Vines hung low, obscuring a clear view in any direction. A thick fog rolled in around Bobby's feet, and he began to hear whispering. There were voices in the mist, gradually getting louder.

Bobby climbed over a mound of jutting asphalt to read a sign above one of the vine-infested buildings. The vines reached out of the front windows like the tentacles of some invisible horrifying monster waiting within. On the front of the building hung an oval sign that read *Duffy Street Seafood Shack*. The paint was entirely faded, and the sign was virtually unreadable, but Bobby could make out the image of a palm tree and a man in a hammock in the center. "How long have we been gone? It couldn't have been more than a year at most. How'd this place fall apart so fast?"

Mac was behind Bobby, climbing up the small mound of broken street.

"The growth of this forest is maybe a hundred years old from the looks of these trees," Mac said. "How is that possible if we've only aged a year?" Bobby asked.

"I think it has to do with the space-time continuum," Mac said.

"Dad, there are large bugs out here. Can we get to civilization, please?" Serena asked.

"There must have been some space-time anomaly when we came back through the cosmic portal, alien egg, or whatever that thing was. I don't think civilization has seen these parts for quite some time, sweetie," Mac said.

"It looks like a war was fought here," Ramos said. He was looking at a muddy, half-submerged human skull resting under a fern. In the center of the forehead was a bullet hole, and half of its upper jae was missing.

"There's more over here," Dante said. "I smell death in the air; something's not right."

Through the trees, piled in a bottomless pit, were the bones and corpses of thousands of people in various stages of decay.

"Oh my God!" Mac said. "This was a massacre," "Or a dumping ground. Not all those corpses are new; some of the bones are sun-bleached with age," Lilith said.

"That's disgusting!" Bobby said.

He stood at the edge of the pit, looking in. The odor, coupled with the sound of millions of flies buzzing, made him ill, and he vomited in front of his shoes. Serena tried to approach and comfort her brother, but Ramos touched her shoulder. "There's nothing you need to see down there," he said.

"Why not allow her to see the reality of unfortunate ends?" Dante said. His head was hurting.

"What's down there can only serve her nightmares," Ramos growled.

"Serena, come back here," Mac said.

Mac looked up and saw something move or shift in the trees, but nothing was there when he focused his eyes.

"We should move on. It looks like we're on what's left of Main Street, and I see a clearing up ahead. Let's go that way," Bobby said.

Mac followed Bobby as he slashed the bushes and weeds out of their way. Dante followed behind him, and

Lilith walked with Mac. Ramos brought up the rear, and Serena walked beside him until she was distracted by a low murmuring behind them. The murmuring became a whisper. She stopped and looked back as Ramos continued without her. "Hello?" Serena asked.

"Sereeeeenaaaa," A voice said. It was a whisper so low it floated on the mist, now gathering around her feet.

"Who's there?" Serena asked.

"Sereeeeena, over here," a child's voice came from the burn pit.

"Where are you? Are you hurt?" Serena asked. Her blond hair caught on a tree branch as she began to walk back through the woods alone.

"I'm stuck!" Serena said. She turned for help, but Ramos was nowhere around. She was alone.

"Serena, come to the edge. I need help getting out." The deeper inflection in his voice told her it was a boy.

"I'm coming!" She untangled her hair and walked through the trees to the edge of the charnel pit.

The pit's stench reminded her of a dumpster full of spoiled meat she had passed by one day after the power went out in her old town. That sickly odor of putrefied flesh permeated her nostrils, and here it was again, but this time, it was people instead of pigs and chickens.

"Over here! You have to come down!" The little boy's voice said. Something moved in the center of the pit, and then she saw the young boy. He was no more than six and looked scared.

"I'm coming, little boy, but this is disgusting!" Serena said. She slid down the dirt wall of the pit, and when she reached the bottom, she saw the partially decayed face of a woman with scraggly, dirt- smeared hair looking up at her through eyeless sockets. The dead were all watching her now. Their agonized faces seemed to be describing their untimely end, pleading from the grave as the worms devoured their bodies. She stepped on one corpse and then another as she traversed the bridge of death.

"Gross," Serena said.

The little boy disappeared as she walked closer to a mound of bodies, but he still called her name. "Are you over there?" Serena asked. There was no answer.

"Serena!" Mac screamed.

He was yelling at her, and suddenly, the spell broken, she realized that she was standing in a pile of rotting bodies. Their odor was on her clothes now, and as she realized there was no boy, Serena turned her head and vomited.

"Daddy!" Serena said.

"Walk back over this way, sweetie!" Mac said.

Dante appeared next to him, and then Lilith.

Mac saw something move in the pit and leveled his rifle at it. By this time, Serena had begun walking back toward the edge of the hole. Dante ripped a vine from one of the trees and threw it down to her so she could use it as a rope. The *something* moved again as Serena was scaling the dirt wall, so Mac took a shot and partially destroyed three bodies piled one atop the other.

"What are you doing in there?" Mac asked. "There was a little boy."

"What little boy?" Mac asked.

The bodies in the pit began to move and squirm behind Serena, rolling over each other as if they were playing a deranged game of Twister.

"Mac, something's coming," Lilith said.

"Yeah, I see it," He shouldered his rifle, looking through the sights.

"Don't look back but climb faster Serena. Please," Mac said.

"I'm coming, Daddy!" Serena said. She was ten feet from the top, and Dante pulled her up as she clutched the vine.

The putrid carcasses of the dead were morphing together to form a massive construct that resembled the shape of a man, with two arms, legs, and a head. The bodies wrapped around in a surreal, connected curve to serve as the head, and through the mouths of the animated corpses came laughter, low and guttural. Mac gasped as the monster stood up, and his head reached the treetops.

"What in god's name is that thing?" Mac said. He squeezed the trigger as Serena cleared the top of the pit.

"It's a corpse monster," Lilith said. "Save my sister!" Bobby said. Mac fired another blue bolt from his rifle and knocked off an arm, but a moment later, it grew the limb back with more bodies and lumbered forward, slapping down at the laser bolts, and flaming arrows. Dante and Lilith drew and loosed their bows, igniting the beast like a torch. It moaned as flames licked the morning air, sending black smoke into the sky as the fat on each body sizzled.

"This type of thing happen when you were here last, Mac?" Dante said.

"No, nothing is the same!" Mac said.

Ramos focused on the dead, listening to their inane chatter. Their voices were a jumble of groans and grunts.

"These wretches have been here for a long time. I can hear their thoughts. This creature is a biological organism, and the people become part of it once thrown on the heap. Their voices are filling my head!" Ramos said.

"Guys, I have no idea how things got this bad. When I left Earth, we were still shooting each other in the streets and blowing up the power grids. There was plenty of chaos, but nothing like the nightmare out there," Mac said.

The monster fell forward, waving its arms around, losing control of the bodies attached to it one after another until the voices inside Ramos's head went silent.

"They all stopped talking," Ramos said. The cavalcade of horrors dropped into the pit, a stinking, flaming mess.

"Dad, I'm sorry. I...I thought someone was hurt in there, and I was trying to help," Serena said. Mac knelt and kissed his daughter on the forehead, then placed his hand behind her head, resting his forehead on hers.

"It's OK, Serena. I can't imagine what I'd do if I lost one of you two," Mac said. Bobby came over and hugged his sister.

A hand reached out of the pit and hooked around Serena's ankle, dragging her back into the fiery pit. Her eyes flashed with shock and desperation as Mac watched his little girl get swept back into the flaming putrescence, they'd pulled her out of only moments earlier. When Serena looked down, she saw the slack-jawed face of an undead man whose skin had been seared black and clung like burned paper to his cheekbones. There were bottomless black pits where eyes once had been, and his rotted mouth was working open and closed as he spoke to her telepathically.

"It's better down here," The man said. "You'll see."

Another hand grabbed her free ankle, and she was pulled back down further into the pit.

"Daddy!" Serena said. She was screaming obscenities at the ghoul attached to her body. Mac leaped into the creature with supernatural speed and crushed its left arm with the force of impact. Serena scrambled free as her wolven father tossed her up and over the side of the charnel pit to safety. The undead began to twitch and vibrate on the burning pile of bodies. The whole pit was ablaze, and the trees were starting to catch fire as Mac pushed off with both feet and performed a backward flip out of the ten-foot-deep pit.

"Heh, that was neat!" Ramos said.

"What was neat? The corpse monster or Serena almost dying, or me flipping out of the pit backward?" Mac asked.

"Well, the first and last thing you just said," Ramos replied.

Mac fired several more rounds into the pit to ensure nothing else was coming out.

"OK, we have to stick together from here on out," Lilith said. "No more going off on your own, little one," Lilith smiled at Serena, and the girl nodded understanding.

"I'm sorry. It won't happen again," Serena said. "Dad, I don't feel like we're on Earth. It's scary here now. I want to go back to Eritria,"

"I know you're scared, but if we all stay together, we will stay alive. Now, let's find out if any locals are left," Mac said.

"You mean, who or what put that thing back there?" Bobby asked. "Yeah, that and how we get a ride out of here," Mac said.

Ramos was wavering back and forth as he stood above the pit of burning bodies.

"Ramos, are you alright?" Dante asked.

"I've not felt right since we came through the portal to this planet. I'm hearing strange voices. This place has a darkness living in it, like a virus, or a plague," Ramos said.

With a loud, squealing scream from the center of the pit, a demon appeared. Standing in the pyre was a nine-foot-tall grey man garbed in black leather armor with a well-muscled physique and long, streaming black hair. His eyes were cobalt blue, and he held a savage two-handed battle sword. He had sweeping black wings upon his back, but they were more like those of a bat than Lilith's feathers. They were leathery and tough.

"You've been gone a long time, Colonel! You should have stayed where you were because this planet belongs to Lucifer now,"

"Who are you?" Mac asked.

"Some call me Azrael, emissary to the Dark Lord. You can call me the angel of death," Azrael said. He laughed mirthfully.

The demon rose out of the pit—hovering—and for a moment, it looked as if he was going shoot into the sky, but as they all watched in silence, the demon became translucent and vanished into the smoke. His jade eyes were the last to disappear, and he winked at Mac just before they vanished.

"Well, that was creepy and psychotic," Mac said. "How did that thing know who you are?" Lilitw said. "Have you encountered it before?"

"No! I have no idea what's going on. None of this makes any sense, and I feel like I'm having an anxiety attack," Mac said.

"I think Dad needs a minute," Bobby said.

"We need to get clear of here and explore the rest of the ruins. I think we'll find answers there," Lilith said.

"The dead here don't make any sense. It's like static inside my head," Ramos said. He gazed into the woods with a dazed, lost expression.

Bobby again led them through the woods, hacking a path out with Ramos's fire sword along Main Street. What remained of the once prosperous vacation spot was nothing more than a few dilapidated buildings obscured by vines, trees, and bushes. Brown leaves crackled and crunched beneath their feet as the team walked. The sun overhead told them it was past noon, and their stomachs were aching for food.

"We need to eat," Dante said.

"I don't smell anything worth eating out here, but I did catch a whiff of something further ahead. We'll need to make quicker progress to get there," Ramos said. He walked ahead of Bobby, raised his hands about five inches apart, palms facing each other, and created a small purple orb. He spread his hands, and the sphere grew larger until it was like a little car.

"Ramos?" Dante asked.

He released the giant ball of purple fire, and it moved forward with a slow, deliberate pace, vaporizing the trees in its path. They did not catch fire and burn; they ceased to be where they had been before and might have ended up in any of a dozen different dimensions. What happened to the trees was one of the most unexplainable occurrences in the life of a small boy named Zenod, who lived in a dimension parallel to that of Mac, who happened to be outside playing along the dirt road leading to his parent's house on a sunny, calm day.

The five-year-old was in a solitary game of Onax raiders versus Xenutians when, for no reason he could ever explain, a row of palm trees appeared in the field. One by one, they materialized in his reality. He gazed at them momentarily, thinking them odd, and then played in the shade they provided for another hour.

Back on Earth, the team was walking along an open trail crafted by their wily warlock with a growing headache.

"Why didn't you just do that sooner?" Bobby asked. Ramos shrugged. "I didn't want to spoil your fun," he said and kept walking.

Lilith rose into the air for a better look around and saw a series of buildings that the jungle had not buried.

"Looks like there might be people up ahead," Lilith said. In the center of a cluster of buildings was a giant black pyramid.

"Let's go there!" Dante said.

Bobby felt the energy of the tablet he carried in his backpack pulsing like an electrical vibration as he experienced an unexplainable power course through his body. The sensation was like tiny fingers working their way up and down his spine, and his head tingled.

"You, OK?" Mac asked him.

Bobby's eyes turned orange and green for an instant as he looked at his father, but the anomaly was gone in a blink, and Mac wondered if he was seeing things.

"Yeah, Dad," Bobby said. "It's just strange, being back here again with so much devastation." Bobby began feeling the grip of supernatural power in his mind as the violet tendrils grew.

Lilith looked to the east and saw a gathering of dark clouds. They encircled a void. She glided back to the ground and joined the others as they walked toward the structure she had seen ahead when, from the bushes, she heard a low rustle, and her ears pricked up.

"What is it?" Mac asked.

"Shhhh!" Lilith said and raised her hand. "There's something..."

Mac raised his rifle in the direction the sound had come from, but Lilith waved for him to lower it. She walked five more steps and knelt, looking carefully into the bushes.

"Who's in there?" Lilith said with a gentle tone and waited. "It's OK; you can come out,"

The leaves and branches of a small bush shivered and parted as two tiny green hands moved them apart.

"Come on out; I won't hurt you," Lilith said, smiling.

"You aren't from around here. Did you come through the portal?" The shaking voice asked.

"We came through *a* portal. I'm Lilith, and these are my traveling companions: Mac, Dante, Ramos, Bobby, and Serena. We seek safe passage to the land called Egypt,"

The tiny creature walked into the light. It was two feet tall, green, standing upright on two spindly legs with a long green spiked tail. The creature's head was small, long, and pointed, looking like a bird with two horns. "You're Lady Lilith?" The creature asked. "The daughter of the lady under the mountain, Ninhursag, has come home again?"

"Do you know me, little one? What are you?" Lilith asked.

"Yes, my lady. My name is Kixle, and I am an imp," Kixle said.

"How do you know about me?" Lilith asked. "You're a legend in many ancient texts, and h long time ago, I researched you while studying the legends of the Anunnaki. We need to move swiftly before the sun sets. Through those trees you just destroyed is the demonic temple of the Ash Brotherhood, and they do not like strangers," Kixle said. His voice was slightly high-pitched and crackled when he spoke.

"How did this happen?" Mac asked.

"I can tell you what I know, but we must be safe. Lady Lilith, would you mind following me?" Kixle said.

"Lady Lilith?" Ramos smirked.

Lilith turned to look at the others, shrugging in confusion. When she turned back, Kixle was gone. He emerged from the branches and waved impatiently for her to follow, giving the others a cursory glance.

"OK, we're coming," Lilith said.

Kixle led them to what, at first glance, appeared to be a massive cave entrance. However, stairs led into darkness under a heavy layer of leaves and broken branches, and Mac recognized it as a maintenance entrance.

"Right this way," Kixle said.

Everyone but the children had to duck under the old cement doorway at the bottom of the stairs and into an underground access tunnel. Dante brought out his light crystal and illuminated the tunnel.

"Put that out unless you want to alert everyone who looks down the manholes above us to know we're down here!" Kixle said.

"How far back does this tunnel go?" Mac asked. "Far enough from the Ash Brotherhood that wa won't have to worry about them storming in and ruining our good time. You are lucky I came out looking for food when I did," Kixle said.

"Did you find any?" Serena asked.

"No. I'm forced to eat whatever the Ash Brotherhood leaves behind. Once the demons ran out of easily hunted people and livestock, they started eating each other. So, I scavenge corpses to survive," Kixle said. He was grumbling to himself in his high-pitched, almost old-man voice.

"You're funny," Serena said. Kixle stopped and looked back at her with yellow eyes that glowed in the dark like tiny flashlights. "Well, maybe not that funny," "We've had a hard time of it here. Earth ain't like the place you left, no way. Demons run amok now, surprised you all ain't seen em',"

Something heavy thundered overhead, shaking loose stones onto the tunnel floor. It sounded to Mac as if a team of giants were pounding the ground with sledgehammers the size of buildings. Kixle stopped moving, and Bobby, behind him, almost fell on top of the imp. Two wide, yellow, glowing eyes scanned the ceiling as Kixle stopped dead and low.

"Shhhhhhh," he said. All movement stopped until the sound was gone. Ahead of them was a round light at the end of their tunnel, but Kixle fixed them all with an eerie gaze in the dark, cramped tube.

"They all come out at night. If you're outside when the demons come, the last thing anyone will hear is your screams," Kixle whispered.

"I'm ready to go back home," Dante said. "Thanks for bringing us here, Mac," Ramos said. "Hey, you two volunteered, and I didn't know, so quit complaining," Mac said. He felt helpless and worse; he'd brought his children back to a world gone, not just sideways, but turned into a nightmare filled with monsters.

"Hell, this place is inside out," Mac whispered. "What?" Lilith asked.

"Sorry, just thinking out loud," Mac said.

"Let's get inside my tunnels where it's safe to speak out loud. Nightfall is coming," Kixle said. Somewhere behind them, another loud pounding above ground shook more loose rubble off the ceiling. Mac looked back with a grimace of disgust and shook his head.

"That sounds like a sane plan to me," Mac said.

Kixle led them into a large cement room held up by sturdy, solid steel supports. Lining the room were mismatched couches of varying lengths and styles. They went around in a circle, and Mac's mind immediately went to hipster bars and lounges where twentysomethings would go to get drunk and listen to house music or maybe even a live band.

Strangely, the decor seemed no less out of place down in the sewer. Victorian-style lamps stood on black glass tables with black, gold thread-lined lampshades adorned with tassels that darkened the light. It really could have been a wonderful place to party, Mac thought. He needed a stiff drink.

"Please, have a seat. Let's chat," Kixle said. As they sat, more eyes peered out of the connecting tunnels. "Come on out; these people mean us no harm,"

Three smaller imps hopped out of the darkness and darted straight for Serena. They stood about a foot tall, looked just like Kixle, and were excited and cheerful to see the little girl.

"Are they going to hurt me?" Serena said. She was backing away with her hands up. "Hah ha! No, not at all. These are my children," Kixle said.

"Oh, OK," Serena said. She smiled at the little green creatures and patted them on their heads.

She allowed them to jump into her arms, and Mac relaxed his finger off the trigger of his rifle. As the imps played with Serena, she giggled playfully with the tiny creatures.

"Do you know how any of this happened?" Mac asked, pointing to the world above the tunnels.

"When the last days of humankind were upon them, some controlled high technology and thought they were gods. They experimented with ways to repair the damage they had done to the planet,"

"How do you know any of this?" Mac asked.

"I just know, alright? When the Earthmen used one of their energy towers, they opened a doorway between this dimension and a dark, hateful dimension next to ours," Kixle said.

"They opened a doorway in space-time, just like your cosmic portal?" Ramos said.

"You mean, the humans let in the ground pounders up above us in the forest?" Lilith asked. "Yes, them and others. Imps and demons alike were set free in this world long ago. Been here ever since." "Well, that's kind of why we're here. We think we can reverse what's happened and put the world bace as it should be," Mac said. "Mac means that we need to get to the land called Egypt. Do you know of any ships or boats that can get us to our destination?" Dante said.

"There ain't been ships in over a hundred years.

What you can do is go through the rift." "What's the rift?" Dante asked.

"It rests between the continents, a tear through space that connects them across the ocean. But, oh, it's dangerous," Kixle said.

"Can you lead us to the opening?" Ramos asked. "You seem like nice people, and I'd hate to see you die."

"Please, we need to get to Egypt, and time is short," Mac said.

Kixle looked at the floor for a moment and then lifted his eyes. "OK, I'll help. We can leave in the morning when it's safer," Kixle said, pointing toward the ceiling.

Something far above them uttered a long, lonely howl as the party looked toward the ceiling and at each other. Dante flexed his claws and growled.

"If we see demons above ground tomorrow, you'd better be prepared to use those," Kixle said.

"Don't worry," Ramos laughed. "He will be."

CHAPTER 4

RAIN WHIPPED THE LONELY BEACH on a chilly day in December 2065, three days before the world's end. Angry ocean waves swelled twenty feet high in the salty air, and petroleum's strong and thick odor permeated the atmosphere.

The waves deposited hundreds of thousands of dead and dying fish and sharks north and south for thousands of miles as the sea died. A whale had been beached about a mile down the shore as frigid wind wrapped around General Thaddeus Longfellow. His thick blond hair lay plastered to his scalp, and the five o'clock shadow of three days past had begun to form a beard. The General's thoughts were heavy as his grey eyes scanned the stormy sea. He desperately wanted a drink and, more importantly, to spend the rest of his miserable life in a bar.

Thaddeus and his team were the last vestiges of DARPA, which stood as technological sentinel against the final apocalypse of man in an age of radical change. Thaddeus thought about the dinosaurs and the peril that came at the end of their millions of years on Earth and wondered if they knew their fate was imminent before the end came. The standard issue waterproof black leather trench coat, resembling the Hugo Boss style worn by SS officers during WWII, kept the beating pellets of water off his uniform, and the upturned collar protected his neck from the worst of the wind.

Thaddeus checked his watch, *twelve twenty-two*, almost time. Twelve thirty, Eastern Daylight Time was the golden hour, and all agents worldwide would activate their towers at the same time. The Tesla tower he stood beside would generate enough electricity from the Earth's waning energetic field and the source field coming from and feeding the universe that the frequency should reach the other towers when their commanders activated the small red button on their control panel.

Static crackled over the walkie-talkie Thaddeus carried in his right hand. He thought of one hand on the comm and one on the red button. He looked at the ocean with sick nausea, watching doom roll in with each wave.

"General, are you ready to go?" Captain Doug Jenkins's voice crackled over the radio.

Thaddeus looked up at the giant tower, a design of inventor Nikola Tesla in the 1920s, looming over his head and wondered if the electrical transmitter would work when he hit the button. "Yes, Captain Jenkins, I'm good to go out here," Thaddeus said.

"I still don't see what you're doing out there, General. If this thing goes sideways, you're getting it first," Captain Jenkins said.

"Well, since the jerks hosting the cosmic portal program failed to come back and get us, it doesn't matter what happens if this thing turns to crap. The world's ending in three days, according to our genius scientists, and I'm standing on a shoreline with the dead and dying results of their predictions right now," Thaddeus said.

"One minute to go, sir. Best of luck to you," Captain Jenkins said.

"May God have mercy on us all, Captain," Thaddeus said.

He looked at his watch as a hammerhead shark rolled in on a swell and landed by his feet. The doomed animal was stomach up, its mouth full of vicious teeth was still working open and closed as thick, black viscous oil from a busted pipeline offshore drained from its gills and onto the sand. It flopped twice on the windswept, rainy beach and then lay still. Thaddeus pressed his button and listened as the low hum of electricity filled the air. All over the world, operators were activating their towers. They were built to repair the energy grid in a final attempt to reverse the damage done to the biosphere. Thaddeus had seen the plans for the towers, and while some of the writing was a mixture of English and Hungarian, there were some strange symbols at the bottom that had never been deciphered by the FBI, CIA, and NSA. Other three-letter acronym agencies from countries around the world willing to play ball with the United States were allowed to see the plans, but none of them knew what the symbols meant.

It was that way for almost a hundred years until a DARPA agent deciphered the letters using his research on ancient Sumerian texts. What Nikola Tesla had written down for future generations was a crafty warning designed to be understood by the highly evolved, just before a consciousness shift into a golden age for man. Unfortunately, only at the end did they finally realize what the mad inventor and mathematician from Hungary was trying to say.

As the Tesla tower generated wild amounts of electricity up and down the coils, dark clouds overhead began to form a funnel from sky to sea. Lightning whirled inside the vortex, and as Thaddeus hoped for a miracle to save humanity, his mind reflected on the translations. They read:

> All life in our universe/multiverse is derived from positive and negative energies. The machine will work on the most prevalent energy. Its use can produce only the most beautiful and dreadful dreams. Humanity will decide which will prevail. The gate is coming.

Thaddeus winced as the sky cracked with an ear-shattering thunder boom. Skillful terrorists had attacked the elite's underground bunkers. Before the three-foot thick missile-proof doors could be shut against them, they breached security and were inside by the thousands, many strapped with atomic weapons, all of them armed. Thousands of miles of underground railways connecting every major city in America were destroyed, and the food production stations, and all life support functions ceased to exist after their staged attack succeeded and doomed the wealthy government officials and elites who had planned to ride out the apocalypse underground. The towers were the last hope for humanity.

"General?" The static whined across the radio. "General, are you alright?" Captain Jenkins said. Something like a dragon's tail poked through the clouds in the tumultuous sky above his head and about a mile out at sea. Thaddeus used his fists to rub his eyes, thinking he saw things, but when he opened them again, beyond the white stars now sparkling in his vision was an exceedingly long tail, whipping in the lightning storm, splashing down into the ocean.

The vortex widened as he stared into the void. The written words, *the gate is coming*, flashed inside his stunned mind. Thaddeus pressed the button again, hoping to turn the tower off as he stood on the beach, surrounded by dead aquatic life, mouth frozen in an O of terror, watching Hell open on Earth. There was no way to reset the switch, and all the towers had coalesced to construct an inter- dimensional bridge.

The adrenaline coursing through his blood abandoned him after the portal opened, and he felt as if he had gone ten rounds with a champion boxer. Suddenly, he felt as if he had no energy left. His feet were planted in the sand as he tried to pick up the radio and respond when he was joined on the beach by the younger, dark-haired man to whom he had just been speaking. Captain Jenkins ran like a man trying to navigate through peanut butter as his legs carried him across the dunes.

"General, are you," Captain Jenkins said when he saw it. "Lord, help us."

The vortex was becoming horizontal and approaching land as the dragon's tail vanished back inside, and a moment later, an enormous three- horned reptile head peered into a darkened world. The swirling clouds touched down on the beach and dissipated like mist, leaving behind an almost translucent bubble that stretched for thousands of miles out into the ocean like a semi-invisible bridge. As the rain poured, they could see the wavering image of what the Tesla towers had just called into being. They had opened something strange, and a void on the other side stretched deep into another world. The general and his captain revered the opening in the sky.

"I think we made a horrible mistake," Thaddeus said.

A second later, a long tentacle came from the opening into this bleak dimension that wrapped around Thaddeus's ankle and whipped him through the air. At first, he felt like he was on an out-of- control amusement park ride, and then the lights went out as he slammed into the same Tesla tower, he had just used to open the interdimensional highway. Captain Jenkins turned to run as his commander's head dropped at his feet.

"Holy crap! This ain't real! This ain't real!" Jenkins screamed.

He turned back to the opening, which was now so large it had parted the clouds, blocked the sunlight, and touched space. Stars winked down upon him as he stood next to General Longfellow's head and gazed into the abyss-like doorway. There was movement inside, and at first, it was wavering, like seeing an image through a kaleidoscope, but then the forms took shape.

Before he could move to do anything else, Army Captain and DARPA employee Doug Jenkins was lanced in the right leg by a long polearm held in the hands of a thirty-foot tall devil man with three horns jutting from his head, two from the sides like a bull, and one from the middle of his forehead. The demon stood above him as more creatures like him rushed through the doorway to Jenkins's world, and then the smaller, imp-like demons bounded through, tossing fireballs in every direction, igniting the sea with their flames.

The more massive beasts had long dog-like maws, pointed ears studded with earrings constructed of skulls, and red leather samurai armor. Jenkins could not understand how these demons' legs worked because they were pointed backward, like the hinges on collapsible ladders. The young captain was lifted into the air and tossed into an oil- soaked flaming ocean, where he dived down, hurt, and terrified, below the waves.

He was terrified, but he swam ferociously toward the doorway that had just opened. If he ran through there and hid, he could get his thoughts together while the monsters ran amok and either vaporized into thin air or came back through when they were done. Either way, it was too dangerous to be on that beach. The fire raged on the water above his head as Doug felt his lungs burn for oxygen. He was drowning, and if he did not get to the gate soon, his lungs would collapse. His leg ached like it was being ripped off as the petroleum-laced salt water entered his wound. He looked down to see green goo leaking from where the polearm had entered his leg. Time was short, but through the flames, he could see the doorway they had opened with the Tesla towers and found an area where the fire had not yet spread on the ocean tide. He swam toward it and lifted his head above the water just enough to breathe. Demons were running all over the beach, and he could hear the tortured screams of people from the nearby town. Thick black smoke rose above the dunes as the city burned, and while Doug was creeping through the doorway, he watched a flying demon carry an old woman out over the ocean and drop her like a hot rock. She flailed with more strength than he would have thought a woman that age should be able to, reminding him of one of those rubbery figures with suckers all over their bodies that you throw and stick to windows. Then she became another piece of driftwood on the tide. The gateway was clear since the demons were busying themselves with the townsfolk, so he ducked down and ran through. It was hot in this new place, filled with sand and big boulders to hide behind.

Inside the new world or dimension or whatever it was, Captain Jenkins eventually found himself alone, exhausted, and in the most pain he had ever been in. The landscape around him was dull and bleak, like a black and white painting of the Arizona desert. Doug located a small cave opening and hop crawled over to it, looking down at the cut in his black uniform trousers. The ooze continued to bubble out of his wound.

"What is that?" Doug asked.

He tried to roll up his pant leg, but the pain was excruciating, and he was beginning to feel waves of nausea rolling over him. Doug looked down at his hands and noticed that the tint of his skin was turning green.

"What the...?" He turned his hands over, and the palms were a lighter shade, and his fingers were more claw-like.

Doug pressed the palms of his hands into his closed eyes to alleviate the pressure pounding behind them. With his eyes closed, he saw the General's face in his mind, the mouth twisted in a death scream as the lifeless eyes gawked up at him on the beach. Thaddeus's glassy eyes had pleaded with him to help, screaming out for one more shot at life, and then the head rolled to the side. Doug closed his eyes for a moment and felt his hands shrinking. When he opened them, to his horror, they were dark green claws with sharp little black nails at the end.

His clothes had grown too large for his body as well, and he was swimming around inside his black combat shirt. Doug felt his face, which was now pointy, like the little creatures he had seen on the beach. His ears were long and sharpened to points, sweeping back from his face. He climbed out of his clothes and looked down to see that the rest of his body had assumed the form of an imp, but the wound on his leg was gone.

"Son of a!!!" Doug screamed.

He had a vision that he had been dropped into a monster movie, and he was the monster. "No way did this just happen," Doug said.

A twenty-foot-tall, overweight demon lumbered by, wearing black steel plate armor, and wielding a telephone pole-sized mace. As he passed, he looked over at Doug, grunted, and continued through the portal to the beach beyond. The demon had left him alone. He was half-relieved to be alive and half- amazed it didn't kill him. Tiny hopping imps dotted the landscape, following the large demons through the inter-dimensional gateway to Earth.

He stood up, stark naked but unashamed in the stale air of this odd world. "I gotta get some clothes that fit," he said.

Doug Jenkins died that day on the beach, and Kixle was born. As the tortured screams of humans filled the air and smoke from demon fires rose, he shook his head and wondered what life would be like now and if it would ever be the same again. Kixle walked away from his human clothes and saw openings in other parts of the planet.

"This place has to be some jumping-off point or a connector between the towers," he said. He could see a Tesla tower outside the portal but had no idea in which country the tower stood. "They've connected it all, or we did."

Kixle bounced to the portal opening, realizing it was more comfortable than merely walking. After the transformation, his legs were like tightly wound springs. He saw another Tesla tower and another one in the other portals. Kixle explored for days as demons all around him came and went, devouring the population of the old world of Earth. The more he thought about what was happening, the more he understood it.

"This dimension must have laid itself right on top of ours," Kixle told himself.

He was surrounded by a barren gray desert on all sides, with villages and towns dotting the land, but about two weeks after his quest began, he noticed a giant black castle in the distance. It was atop a cliff overlooking a frozen ocean, and as he drew closer, several large tentacles erupted out of the sand, tossing him to the side. The arms whipped in the air and grew longer as something under the sand emerged. The monster rose high above Kixle, who stood with his mouth open, unsure if this would be his final day. It looked like a large terrestrial octopus with fangs and beady eyes recessed under a broad brow ridge and had a slightly humorous cartoon look. Ringed with knife-sharp needles, the suckers on its tentacles were perfect for grabbing prey, and this removed some of the humor.

"What do you want, imp?" the monster asked. It cast an annoyed gaze upon Kixle.

"I, uh, I was just headed..."

"You know the boss doesn't have time to fool with you little guys. Archdemons and above *only* can get access to the master," The monster growled. Its voice was like an angry drill sergeant.

"Right, uh, my mistake. I'm heading out to heck up some humans anyway," Kixle said.

"That's the idea. Get out there and have fun.

And imp..."

"Yeah?" Kixle asked.

"You come back here again, and I'll toss you into the lava pools," The monster said.

"Sure, no problem. I'm gone," Kixle said. The monster burrowed below the surface and vanished, leaving a relieved and terrified green imp alone in the barren desert.

The sheer lack of color affected his ability to gain visual perspective, and he felt that if he stayed in there for any length of time, he might go mad. The desert went on in every direction for an eternity, but now there were cliff faces and ancient ruined buildings.

"Where am I?" Kixle asked. Mac woke from the dream. In the darkness of the tunnels, he was uncertain what time it was, but he suspected that he would have to speak with Kixle.

"Colonel MacDonald, come with me," Kixle said. He was whispering while everyone else slept. Dante was snoring, occasionally giving a yip, and kicking his legs. Mac had a dog that would do that when he was a kid, and he always assumed she was chasing rabbits or cats in her sleep, but he figured that Dante was pursuing thirty-foot-tall monsters with rows of razor-sharp teeth.

Mac stood and located the imp's tiny yellow eyes as he turned to lead Mac down an adjacent tunnel. Mac followed in silence until they arrived at another maintenance room, illuminated by candles on shelves about four feet off the floor.

"What's up, Kixle?" Mac asked.

"You tell me. You said my real name while you were sleeping. How do you know what my old name is?" Kixle asked.

"Just a vivid dream, but I'm guessing it was no dream. I saw a man on a beach, and there was a doorway to another dimension, and then he changed into, well..." Mac said.

"Yeah, the glorious form you see before you was a blessing and a curse given to me the day these darn demons arrived. I should thank them; this has kept me alive this long," Kixle said. "If that dream was right, it's been a hundred and fifty years since the Tesla towers opened that gate. How are you still alive?" Mac asked.

"That's true; it was one-hundred and fifty-two years ago. And I concluded, after a lot of time thinking, that these creatures must have an unnaturally long life. Some of them have been alive for millions of years. I suspect that as long as I keep my head attached, I'll live for an exceptionally long time," Kixle said.

"You ever think about ending it? I honestly didn't mean that to sound like it did; it's just that you've been around a long time, you know?" Mac asked.

"Used to, but not anymore. You'd be amazed at what you can get used to if you live long enough, and about five years after this happened to me, I realized that maybe I'm here for a grand purpose," Kixle said.

"A grand purpose?" Mac asked.

"Yeah, to live long enough to see you come back and repair the crap we did to this planet all those years ago," Kixle said.

"You know who I am?" Mac asked.

"You're Colonel Derrick MacDonald, supposed savior of humanity. I know the story, but you failed. Most of humanity died horrifically fighting and ultimately dying in the fire pits of monsters from another dimension," Kixle said. "I had no idea how bad it had all gotten when we were gone, but you have to know I tried. Truly," Mac said. Kixle seemed tense, and Mac wondered what to do if things became violent.

"Go on; you've suffered some condition that turned you into a wolf, so you're not untouched by the reality of our situation. I've waited a century and a half to see you return, the one man I've hated all this time," Kixle said.

"To us, me and the kids, we've only been gone about a year, but something happened when we came back through, and I suppose we ended up in your time because of it. I went on a mission to the planet Eritria to open the cosmic portal back to Earth, and when we could do that, only a handful of elites came across. I had no control over that decision, but we did cut them off from ever being able to get back here. The hell of it is I lost most of my crew over this, and the General who sent us died in my arms," Mac said.

"What made you come back?" Kixle asked. "I had a vision that we could return and fix the world, but I needed to get to Egypt. I was on a ship, and our artifact on Eritria can help fix this mess. So, I staked our future on that vision and risked my children's lives," Mac said.

"I'd laugh if what you told me wasn't so sad. You were free of this place, and you came back?

"I suppose I did," Mac said. Kixle shook his head. "Anyway, what was this Eritria like?" Kixle asked.

"It was a beautiful, wild place full of adventure and intrigue. It was as if we had landed on Earth a million years ago when the population was so small you could walk for a week and never see another soul. The air was so fresh and clean that the atmosphere was pure. The people there are strange and fascinating, and I immediately fell in love with them," Mac said. His head hung low.

"Paradise lost, huh? Well, let's go there. I'm dead serious, Mac. You and your children can only die here on what Earth has become," Kixle said.

"Yeah, that'd be great, but the first night we arrived here, an ET landed and took the cosmic portal. It turns out it was some egg for its kid. I thought we were going to die out there on that beach, but it left us alive. After the baby hatched, they took off in a spaceship. Dante, Ramos, and Lilith are stranded here, and two of my crew are stranded on Eritria," Mac said.

Kixle leaned back against the wall, shaking his head in disgust. "This just gets better and better, Colonel,"

"It is what it is, but if you can help us, we still might be able to fix things. I didn't come all this way not to succeed now," Mac said.

"I'm guessing you had an army behind you back there?" Kixle said. "We did," Mac said.

"You have me, my kids, and the six of you for this little reckoning. How do you think we'll pull it off? As far as I can tell, the dimension that overlaid ours isn't the biblical Hell, but the wordsmiths and painters weren't far off in their depictions of Hell's minions. These guys are nasty, evil, and love to skewer anything they can get their hands on; that ain't one of them,"

"I thought there might be humans in the town above us," Mac said.

"Sure, there are pockets of humans here and there, but the monsters got most of em' a long, long time ago. The

Ash Brotherhood is all that lives up there now," Kixle said. He pointed up.

"The demons turned you into an imp. Could they have done the same to others?" Mac said.

"If they did, the others would have been good at concealing it, or maybe they moved on. Who knows, right? I've been alone here without a mate or companionship for over twenty-five years. The kids are my only outlet, so I suppose they're my companions, but darn it's lonely," Kixle said.

"What happened to their mother? If you don't mind me asking," Mac asked.

"No, mother. It turns out imps are asexual. They're all mine, and I have one about every ten years or so," Kixle said. "You said you've been alone for twenty-five years. So, there was someone, right?" Mac asked.

"She was a true imp and never forgave the fact that I'm a hybrid," Kixle said. "Ahhh, she was fun," He looked away with a longing stare as a man remembering a better day.

"My girlfriend is a succubus, and I'm not going to compare notes, but she's not disappointing either," Mac said.

"What are you two talking about?" Lilith said. She ducked into the room, shot Mac a knowing glance, and sat on the floor next to him. He kissed her on the cheek. "Uh-huh," she said.

"Whoops, busted," Kixle said, laughing.

Kixle told her his story, Mac shared his dream, and the three talked until dawn. Kixle even laughed a few times, and by the time the sun had come upon a brand-new day, their party had expanded by four.

CHAPTER 5

BOBBY WOKE UP SOMETIME AFTER Mac and Kixle disappeared down the tunnel. Even with Serena on one side and Ramos on the other, he was freezing. The ancient sewer tunnel had been warm and dank when they had entered, almost sticky with humidity, but now it was like winter next to the wolven warlock.

Bobby reached inside his backpack, and a quantum battery-powered flashlight was in one of the smaller pockets. He took it out and clicked the small light on. Ramos was sleeping with his back to the children and grunting with an almost imperceptible, low growl. Bobby shined the light over Ramos and could feel the cold coming off him as if a freezer door had been opened. His breath blew out in tiny, wispy clouds in the beam of Bobby's flashlight.

"Bobby?" Serena said.

She was propped on her elbow, lying on the musty old couch cushions Kixle had given them to sleep on. Bobby waved a hand at her to be quiet, and when he looked back, Ramos was staring at him with a dreadful purple glow in his eyes. A sinking feeling nagged in Bobby's stomach like they were all sitting in quicksand.

"Are they still alive? Are we there yet?" Ramos said. He was looking past Bobby as if the young man were not there.

"R, Ramos? Are you alright?" Bobby asked. He felt his pulse quicken, and for the first time since he had met the wolven, Bobby was afraid of one.

"Bobby, are you..." Serena said. "I'm fine. Ramos, are you awake?" Bobby asked. "What? Oh, uh, yeah, I'm fine. Just a bad dream,"

Ramos said.

The purple light faded, and Bobby felt the temperature in the room return to normal, but his sense of fear remained.

"What happened to you?" Bobby asked. "You were so cold. It was like sleeping next to an open window in winter,"

Ramos had a dreamy, distant, troubled look in his eyes. "I don't know. I was walking along a mountain pass back home, and then I tumbled into a frozen abyss," Ramos said.

"Do you feel...OK?" Bobby said.

"No, I don't think I've been well since..." His voice drifted away, and he stared into the ceiling. "...we came through that cosmic portal of your fathers," Ramos said.

Mac heard Bobby speaking and entered the room where they had all been sleeping to get them up for breakfast.

"Is everything OK?" Mac asked.

"Ramos was as cold as a block of ice a minute ago," Bobby said.

"I'm not sure what happened, Mac. I haven't felt right since we crossed over into your world. I need to return home," Ramos said. He was holding his head. "You don't look well, my friend, and if I can return you to your home, it will be done. I'm sorry this is happening to you," Mac said.

"I don't know what it is, but I'm beginning to feel less like me and more like a monster," Ramos said and shook his furry head, never finishing his statement.

"I know what you mean; I've been having a recurring dark dream about a gate. It's this wrought iron horror, and I can see through to the other side, but the land is bleak, dying, and I get the sense that it's calling to me. I can also see the faces of the dead, the victims of that USAP that got us to Eritria," Mac said, trailing off.

"When I'm dreaming, I keep walking through the same gate, and Mom's there. She's in a land of green grass surrounded by trees and flowers, and she's smiling at me," Bobby said.

"I saw mom, too. Same dream as Bobby," Serena said.

"I'd rather dream about that instead," Mac said.

Kixle had rations in his pseudo-pantry, and there was enough for everyone to fill their bellies before going out into the light of a new and uncertain day. Kixle had managed to get a wooden dinner table down there, and as they all sat around on rickety chairs eating unidentifiable meat, he ushered his bouncing little green children into the room. "Daddy!" They all chimed at once. Kixle laughed as the three of them hopped around him with childish glee. He hugged all three and pointed toward a hunk of meat on a butcher block. "Go eat; we have to be on our way soon. I'm taking them to the tower,"

The hungry party tore into their breakfast, eager to get back on track and end the mystery of Mac's dream of Egypt.

"So, you came back here to repair the Earth, but how exactly are you planning on doing this?" Kixle said.

Mac looked up from his meal. "It involves the Great Pyramid of Giza; we have to get there. According to my vision, that is,"

"You need to cross the ocean? Aside from going through that portal and crossing the desert, I don't know of a way monsters control the seas now, and I don't think a ship has run in over a hundred years. Unless you count the sky pirates, they're all rusted hulks by now, but they're reclusive and combative. I don't even know if they exist anymore," Kixle said.

"Well, we have to find a way," Mac said.

"It's a suicide mission, Colonel. I'm not saying I'm not with you or that I don't support your vision, but the things that live here now are a one-way ticket to the afterlife," Kixle said.

"We're the only ones left to do it unless you're hiding an army somewhere around here," Mac said. "I'll give you this; you must have some great power to have gone through everything you say and survived to tell the tale," Kixle said.

"Can you get us to Egypt, Kixle? It's been a long time since we've seen normal life, and it'd be good to have this over with," Bobby asked.

"You'll have to go through one of the dimensional portals; over the last sixty years or so, they've been malfunctioning. The demons use those to get around, but they have no idea how to fix the towers when they stop working," Kixle said.

"So, what are they, like light switches that click on and off?" Mac asked.

"Kind of, but it's more like the picture on a TV screen coming in and out; only you can enter the TV, and if you happen to catch it when it's on the way out of focus, you'll be atomized," Kixle said. He lowered his face, shaking his head.

"Is that the tower I saw down on the beach yesterday? Something was shimmering near it that looked like a mirage," Mac said.

"That's the closest Tesla tower, and the gate next to it is one of the ones that comes and goes. If you cross into it while it shimmers, die. I've seen it happen before, but not for a long time. Sixty years back, some human took off down the beach to escape from one of the flying imps and ran straight into the gate while the tower malfunctioned. I watched him pixelate and vanish as he screamed. That was also the last human I saw in these parts until you all showed up," Kixle said.

"So, we're taking our chances either way, and demons may attack us," Ramos said.

"Well, we can't just sit under here forever. No offense, Kixle," Bobby said.

"None taken, but it's worked very well for me," Kixle smiled.

"Look, if we get down there and you see a gray desert landscape, we can cross. Otherwise, we'll have to find another tower if we see nothing. I know the towers were installed up and down the coast, in one-hundred-mile intervals by my DARPA cohorts, back before it all went to the dogs," Kixle said. "DARPA? How do you know about them if you're an imp, Kixle?" Bobby asked.

"It's a long story; ask your dad," Kixle said and got up. Mac waved a dismissive hand at his son and shook his head.

"A lot's changed since we left. Let's say that some interesting developments occurred in the last days of the previous age," Mac said.

"Let's get moving if nobody else has objections," Mac said.

The party followed Kixle and his bouncing children through one long, dark tunnel after another until they came to an opening where daylight shone through. After spending a night in the tunnels, the circle of light was almost blinding, but as they emerged to a brand-new day, they found themselves standing in a forest of tall trees surrounding the ruins of a former city. Brick buildings jutted out of the sandy soil like broken teeth, almost obscured by the overgrowth of vines. Mac walked next to Kixle.

"Yesterday, when we were walking through the woods after leaving the beach, we were confronted by a giant corpse-monster," Mac said.

"That's the undying pit you ran across. Demons constructed it, and whatever goes in never fully decays," Kixle said.

"Yeah, it was disgusting in more ways than one. But after we fought it and won, a gray-winged man who knew me by name appeared. He called himself Azrael. Do you know who that was or why he'd know who I am?" Mac asked.

"No idea, Mac. You are dealing with the supernatural realm now, where nothing is as it seems. Not anymore. The minute we operated those Tesla towers, we damaged the fabric of reality on this planet. We created a nightmare we could not repair, and it all fell in a domino effect. And now the forces at work here are difficult to understand," Kixle said.

"I get it, but it just seemed odd and slightly frightening that a man who can vanish—*at will*— would know who I am when I haven't been on this planet for a hundred and fifty years," Mac said. "If you think that's odd, just wait until you've had a run-in with the faeries," Kixle said.

"Did you say faeries?" Ramos asked. He pushed his way forward and stood over Kixle with wide eyes.

"Yes, the faeries have been here longer than modern humans have, but they're strange folk and don't often deal with men. Well, not in a waking manner, anyway. They tend to come while people are sleeping and do...things in a sexual manner," Kixle said.

"Faeries, come and have sex with you while you're sleeping? Alright," Bobby said. Mac rolled his eyes, and Dante snickered.

"It's not a pleasurable experience, from the accounts I heard long ago. They paralyze their victim, do their thing, and then extract your, you know, to take back to their holes underground. I've heard it can be an overwhelming and terrifying experience, Kixle said.

"Oh, sounds fun," Bobby said.

"Dante, the faeries might be able to take us home," Ramos said. He looked over at Dante, and he seemed himself again for the first time since coming through the cosmic portal.

Something rattled in the trees, and a second later, Dante was flying like a tossed beanbag. He had no time to react, and the contents of his stomach ejected from his mouth as he glided through the air and crashed into a tilting palm tree. He slid to the ground, shaking his head as Mac landed beside him. It was a thirty-foot-tall giant, and it had discovered them coming out of the tunnel.

Ramos was already screaming in rage as Serena ran for cover. Lilith saw the shape moving toward her and dodged out of the way, instinctively shooting a fire bolt from her hand. Her fire struck an enormous leg that almost kicked Bobby, had he not dodged at the last second, and tumbled across the ground. The fire sword he had borrowed was still in his pack.

He rolled painfully across the roots of a tree and some medium-sized rocks to reach into the backpack and retrieve Ramos's sword. The giant was walking past, seeming not to notice him on the ground when he held the grip tightly and watched with satisfaction as a beam of fire thrust forth. As the giant passed by, Bobby slashed it in the Achilles heel of each foot and dodged quickly behind a tree.

The monster's legs suddenly looked like an upside-down Pez dispenser, and it could no longer support its weight. The giant's legs buckled, and it toppled to the ground with a thump, but on its way down it broke half a dozen trees and trapped Dante beneath it, pinning his arms to the ground.

"Crap! I'm trapped!" Dante said, howling.

He tried to pry himself out by raising the giant's leg with his unpinned legs and torso, but his position was awkward, and he could not budge it. Bobby tried to help Dante and ran around to where his friend was pinned, but as he got under the meaty leg, the beast's sheer weight struck him, and an offensive odor wafted from its armpits.

"I can't budge it, Dante!" Bobby said. He tried several distinct positions and grips, but it was no use. Down, but not out, the giant swiped a hand backward and hit Lilith from behind as she tried to get Mac to his feet. The injured enormity was attempting to get to his feet as the ripped Achilles tendons in his legs hung free and green blood poured from the open wounds. He grunted in pain and reached back to grab Dante in his powerful grip, knocking Bobby to the ground. The teen landed painfully on a rock, a sharp edge wedging itselk between his butt cheeks.

"Yeeeeooowwwww!" Bobby yelled. He rolled over on his side, both hands covering his damaged posterior as Dante was lifted through the air in the clutches of their injured foe.

"Well, at least I'm free from that leg," Dante said, dangling from the giant's fist.

Seeing his son was hurt, Mac ran back and helped him to his feet.

"Are you alright?" Mac asked.

"Yeah, but my rear end feels like someone hit me with a bat," Bobby said. A dark stain formed in the center of his jeans as he fought to stand. Kixle squinted upward and saw that the demon had two horns on its head and a pig-like face. Lilith shot her bow and put a sizable hole in the giant's right wrist. As the gap widened and showed daylight through the other side, it dropped Dante, whose adrenaline sent abnormal strength to his muscles. He struggled to his feet as the monster's knee hit him in the ribs, and he was caught beneath the creature's meaty thigh. It pinned his arms, and he was trapped. More monsters could be heard thundering through the trees, and as they broke through to the clearing, Ramos turned around and raised his hands. Mac could hear the sounds of the beach; it was close, and he thought they could make it if they could get to the coast. As the thought went through his mind, a falling limb crashed down on his head, knockinf him unconscious.

Ramos walked forward, hands raised, as two large purple orbs danced on his fingers, growing larger by the minute. Three pig giants rushed through the trees but were toppled backward as Ramos thrust his purple fire in their direction. One of the pig-man- giants looked down to see that a massive hole had been ripped through his midsection; the other two creatures were missing arms and legs. Ramos moved forward, rage growing. The fire in his eyes danced six inches from the sockets like blowtorches, and when he held his hands up again, a vibratory force field surrounded him. He waited until he could no longer control the energy, allowing it to slip from his fingers. The ensuing pulse wave destroyed trees in a fifty-yard-wide path through the forest.

"Everybody, get out of here!" Ramos shouted over the screams of an onslaught of enemies.

Demonic forces of all shapes and sizes rushed the small band of warriors.

Mac woke up with a splitting headache in time to see Bobby running up the monster's back, fighting the pain in his rear end as the blood blossom grew larger. An involuntary thought flashed through Mac's mind as he watched his son climb the giant. The kid was going to need stitches in his butt, and there would be nothing fun about the next few weeks for him.

Dante used his superior animalistic strength and struggled free, ripping several fingers from the giant's hand in his escape. Bobby ignored the pain, and his feet carried him along the giant's solid spine as he balanced himself while running.

"Ungh! Gonna kill all of you! Eat your bones!" The giant said. He was bellowing in pain because of his torn ankles.

The giant struggled to stand up as Bobby gripped his sword and slashed the back of its neck, severing the spine with an expert blow. The giant pigman hit the ground with a thud and stopped moving. Kixle had scanned the area for his kids when Ramos screamed for them to evacuate, but they were nowhere to be found.

"Dwee! Kimble! Sasha!" Kixle said. He was bouncing around, fearful of Ramos's warning for them to escape.

He had to assume the children had made it to the beach, so he hurried down to the shore. "Bobby! Let's go! Serena, come on!" Mac said.

He motioned toward the ocean, pausing to see the strain on Ramos's face.

"Coming, Dad!" Serena said. She was already running ahead of them, half out of her mind with terror, and she could see the waves rolling in through the dense trees.

Mac looked at Ramos again, and he knew from the strain on his face that whatever magic the warlock held back was about to pop, and he didn't want to be around for the outcome. Mac looked around and made sure his children were ahead of him as he ran through the woods toward the shore. Dante joined him, sidling up beside them while they ran.

"It's about time. I saw you back there laying down on the job," Mac said.

"Hey, what do you want? I was held up," Dante said. He had a smirk on his face.

"Dante, ladies and gentlemen...he's here all week. Tip your servers," Mac said.

The two warriors darted toward the sea as Ramos returned to the hordes. He had never seen such creatures, even in the darkest recesses of Eritria. Some demons resembled spiders with human faces; others were impish, like Kixle. The more massive demons were heavily armored and came in varied sizes. There were skeletal warriors, more giant pig men, and dog-faced soldiers, and in the back, floating among them, Ramos could see their spell crafters. Cloaked figures with glowing blue eyes levitated above the army.

Ramos judged they were about twenty yards from him, and he felt his energy growing. Something about this world was changing him, and at the same time, his thoughts were becoming darker, and he was becoming more powerful. His body hummed like an electrical transformer, and the bubble grew, igniting bushes and scrub grass at his feet. Fifteen yards, twelve, eleven, then Ramos looked up, and with the fury of a thousand jungle creatures, he unleashed his rage.

A powerful blast of heat and pressure exploded, mowing down the onslaught of supernatural beings. "Aaaaaaghhhhhhhhh! I cannot control it!" Ramog said.

He was screaming and speaking in languages he was confident he had never been taught as he turned the woods into a nightmarish hellscape of smoldering demons. The army was on fire, and those closest to Ramos were liquefied by the heat, each layer of fat melting like candle wax and adding to the blaze. The spell crafters were on fire and drifting into the flame-engulfed trees. Ramos could have spent the day fighting the hordes, but he urgently needed to get to the beach. He used his warlock ability to raise the deceased, scorched giants from their graves and turn them on the other approaching demons. He heard someone in the back booming with a commanding voice.

"Don't let them escape! Kill them all!" The man's voice commanded.

Ramos recognized the figure as the gray, winged man they had seen at the charnel pit the day before.

"Azrael," Ramos said.

He commanded his undead to knock a row of trees over, efficiently blocking their path and allowing him time to break free. Ramos turned and ran the way his friends had, leaping over the dead giant as he went. He could hear the screams of the burned and dying and over it, all the voices of their winged commander screaming for them to kill. Ramos ran onto the beach and joined the others as they stood by the leaning, rusted Tesla tower, and stared into a shimmering, bubble-like gateway. The desert world flickered like a strobe: ocean, desert, ocean, desert.

"Ramos, did you see my kids in there?" Kixle asked.

"No, sorry. I only saw a horde of demons. After I set the forest on fire, nothing could survive it. They'll have to find another way around unless they're fireproof. Do we have an escape plan, or are we swimming?" Ramos asked. Kixle lowered his head in mourning.

"They would have come out here by now, or they would have stayed next to me. I have to find them," Kixle said.

"That's suicide. You go back in there, and they'll kill you for helping us, or you'll die in the fire," Ramos said.

Kixle gave them all one last desperate look and bounced away into the fiery woods. Black smoke rose over the treetops as the ancient buildings burned along the forest. The last any of them saw of Kixle was his little green body bounding over a rotted log and into the burning trees.

"The gate's not working, and in a few minutes, about a million of those demons are gonna flood this beach. It was nice knowing all of you," Dante said.

From overhead, a woman shouted, "Hey, you down there! Climb the ladder, and let's go!"

They looked up to see a metal train car with the words A *trak* painted on the side. Significant patches of rust were shown through the gray paint, and a giant balloon suspended the vehicle. It was covered with a black material that was a shield of some sort. Jet engines glowed white hot as they hung in the air about fifty feet above their heads. Next to A *trak* were more letters spray-painted in the fashion of a poorly trained graffiti artist and read *Deezil*. Rocket engines were bolted to the back of each side, and aircraft wings were attached to the middle. To Mac, the defunct Amtrak train car looked like the funky creation of an enormous, inventive child.

Steel plates covered the windows, and cannons had been installed on the roof. One large cannon barrel stuck out of a porthole and was aimed at the beach.

"Make a decision, people! Now, or we jam out!" The voice boomed. A chain ladder dropped down from the bottom of the *Deezil* onto the beach. It led upward into the interior of the train car.

"Let's go!" Mac said.

He pushed Serena toward the ladder first, Bobby next, and then he and Dante followed them up. They followed her up as shouts and curses from the demonic army in the forest grew louder. Lilith flew up and perched herself on the train car's roof, standing guard in case anything came rushing out of the woods before her friends were safe. Finally, Ramos climbed up last. Mac entered the train car and first noticed the overwhelming fragrance of hydraulic fluid and body odor.

He saw that the walls were lined with what may have once been comfortable couches when they were new but now looked like the kind of thing someone would find in an online gamer's basement—ratty, old, and covered with odd, unidentifiable stains. Mac's vision adjusted to the low light as Lilith entered the portal, and the *Deezil* floated away from the beach. While Bobby felt the beneficial energy of the tablet against his back, he realized that his busted derriere was fixed.

"Welcome aboard the *Deezil*, everyone. I'm Jasmine, the captain of this rig," A female voice said. Mac turned toward her in the dim light of a string of LED Christmas bulbs. He saw a beautiful woman with long dark hair, chestnut skin, and pretty, high cheekbones. Jasmine looked to be in her mid- thirties, and she was dressed in jeans, black calf-high leather boots with a red-checkered flannel shirt, and a black pirate patch over her left eye. "Now, who are you?" She asked.

CHAPTER 6

"**H**ERE GOES, MY NAME IS Colonel Derrick MacDonald, U.S. Air Force, Special Operations. I was part of an unacknowledged special access project around 150 years ago that was sent on a mission to save humanity. But you can call me Mac," He put an arm around Serena and a hand on Bobby's shoulder. "These are my children,"

"I'm Bobby," Bobby said. "Serena," Serena said. "I'm Lilith," Lilith said.

"My name is Ramos of the Blood Paw wolven on the planet Eritria," Ramos said.

"I'm Dante, Ramos's better-looking and younger brother," Dante said.

"A hundred and fifty years? Bull!" Jasmine said, furrowing her brow. "One thing we don't do is lie to each other on this craft. Liars get people killed, and there are precious few of us left for shenanigans. Dominic, let's drop them off over the ocean," She reached for a gun on her belt. "No, it's true!" Bobby said. "Look,"

He removed his backpack and dug inside one of the pockets, retrieving a small, dirty, white plastic card with a picture of his face. Jasmine took it from him and looked it over.

"It's my high school ID card. Look at the date," Bobby said.

Her eyes widened. "This reads 2058, but there's no way you could be this old. You're a kid. Did you come through one of those demon portals? Are you a demon?" Jasmine asked. Her voice was shaking a bit as the card in her hand trembled.

"No, Jasmine, we're not demons," Mac said. He transformed back into a man.

"Holy crap! How'd you do that? Trexler! Dex!

Get up here," Jasmine shouted.

Two men came running from a room at the back of the car. They were dressed in jeans, T-shirts, and leather dusters, like the kind cowboys in the old West might wear. The taller one was white with a full beard and covered in grease; he carried a pipe wrench. His T-shirt had a skateboard emblem silkscreened onto it with the faded words *Treehouse* written across the middle of his chest. The smaller of the two had brown skin and looked to be of Indian descent.

His facial hair was more of a five o'clock shadow edging on full beard strength. He was skinny, wore coke bottle glasses, and tried to look dangerous with a ball peen hammer in his right hand. He held it shoulder height at the strangers, and Mac might have been intimidated had it not been for the fact that his T-shirt read *Who needs big boobs when you have a butt like this.*

"What's the problem, Captain?" The tall man said.

"Dex, these guys are..." Jasmine said. "Everybody stop!" Dante roared. Jasmins stopped talking, and everyone looked at him. "Go ahead, Mac. Explain,"

"I participated in a project that was supposed to save the people of Earth a long time ago. We captured an alien spacecraft and a device that could open portals through space-time. We were supposed to colonize a new planet, open the portal back to Earth, and allow the rest of the humans to come across. That's what we were told before we left.

However, after losing half my crew and surviving a war against mythical creatures, we were able to open the cosmic portal back to Earth. What came through weren't the hordes of rescued people we expected, however, but an ultra-wealthy group of elitists and their hired army of paramilitary contract killers. Because the people of Eritria were good to us, we couldn't allow the rest of the humans to wipe everyone out," Mac said. "And how did you return here a hundred and fifty years later?" Jasmine asked. Dex and Trexler had already lowered their makeshift weapons.

"I don't know exactly. It was related to time relativity, as time can go by differently on different planets. All I know is that we spent about a year on Eritria, and then over a century had passed by the time we came home. Who are you if you don't mind my asking?" Mac asked.

The taller of the two, whom Mac was already beginning to think of as Mr. Pipe Wrench, spoke first. "I'm Dex, and the little guy is Trexler," Trexler said, standing with his mouth agape beside his taller partner.

"What did you say your name was?" Trexler asked.

"Mac, Colonel Derrick MacDonald," Mac said. "Hold on one second!" Trexler said. He was on the verge of hyperventilating and ran back to the room from which he and Dex had emerged, mumbling something about a book.

"So, you expect me to believe this story," Jasmine said. She glared through her good eye until Trexler bounded back into the room.

"Right here!" Trexler said. He opened a leather- bound book that looked like it had been unearthed from an ancient tomb. "You're famous, man!"

He flipped to a page with news article clippings from a magazine titled *The Enquirer* taped to it, and Mac leaned over to get a better look. When he saw what Trexler was holding, his jaw dropped.

"Holy crap, you've got an *Enquirer* article from the year twenty-sixty-one," Mac said. He whispered the words.

"It's you, isn't it?" Trexler said.

The article was titled AIR FORCE COVER UP – TIME TRAVEL – NOW POSSIBLE!!! and in the article, the reporter mentions a Colonel Derrick MacDonald and a few other officers he served with, along with the spacecraft they flew to a planet called Eritria on, and a device that opened portals in space- time. The article described a top-secret project planned by a rogue element of the military designed to find life on other planets and open portals in space-time. It reported that an elite group of power barons from global corporations had funded the project and that their plans did not include rescuing the majority of humanity. The words were written at the top of the article in black marker: *Conspiracy theory?*

"This is pretty accurate. I don't know how they got this story, but I'm *sure* the poor son of a bitch who drafted the article was dead the day after it went to print," Mac said.

A photograph on the right of the article showed Mac standing with General Martin at an awards ceremony. Their names were listed from left to right, and Mac was only a little surprised to see *Colonel Derrick MacDonald* printed in bold black letters. Jasmine walked over to look and began nodding her head, the sides of her mouth turned down in a frown of acknowledgment.

"Well, it seems we're in the presence of ancient time travelers. Where's the device you used to get back to Earth?" Jasmine asked.

"Gone. It disappeared the night we got back and subsequently left my friends, the wolven, trapped here,"

"Don't forget about me!" Lilith said. She looked at him with an indignant grimace.

"How could I ever, you won't let me," Mac grinned. "Yeah, Lilith, too."

He walked over and kissed her on the lips. She looked at him sideways for a second, pulled her head back, and then allowed it.

Bobby looked out of one of the heavily armored portholes.

North Myrtle Beach was ablaze as the *Deezil,* and her new passengers escaped the inferno flying out over the Atlantic Ocean. Towering columns of black smoke rose into the morning sky like angry storm clouds. As high as they were, Mac could still recognize some of the old city and the highways. What he saw was like the nightmarish apocalyptic aftermath of every global war film he had ever watched or heard of. Some of the hotels remained along the coast, but few, and those that did stay were jutting out of the sand in weird angles, like the broken dreams of all those who perished when the deadly tsunami washed them away. Bobby could see twenty or thirty large demons storming the beach where they had been minutes before through one of the cannon portals. A shiver tickled his spine.

"Maybe this is how it was the last time man ruled the Earth," Bobby said. He mumbled and hadn't seen Dex sidle up on his right side.

"The last time the world was destroyed may have been when a massive planet called Nibiru, or planet X, orbited too close to the Earth. The gravitational pull of that world caused planetwide tsunamis on Earth that washed away most of the old world, including a lot of the advanced technology," Dex said.

"I heard it was because of a comet," Bobby said. Volleys of arrows soared through the air, narrowly missing the *Deezil* as the beach filled with demonic archers.

"OK, Dominic, let's get the heck out of here!" Jasmine shouted to the front.

"Yes, dear!" Dominic shouted. His voice sounded far away and distant to Bobby.

"After the cataclysm, they were so devastated that it took more than twelve thousand years to figure out what happened to them, and what we know of our ancestors is probably only a small percentage of the facts. Some of the important stuff was dug up in places like Egypt, South America, and Indonesia, but that was back before we let the world fall apart," Trexler said. He was standing on Bobby's left side.

"Pardon me if this sounds odd, but how do you know any of that?" Bobby asked. Trexler let out a good-natured chuckle.

"Doesn't sound odd at all, and I apologize for rambling, but we don't get many visitors. I'm what you might call a fan of history and the plight of man, so when I'm not helping my brother Dex here fix this rig, I'm in search of lost libraries and the mysterious tomes contained within," Trexler said. Bobby turned to Dex and read his T-shirt, chuckling to himself.

"I always heard it was because a comet melted the ice sheet and devastated the planet. I'm Bobby; pleased to meet you," He stuck out his right hand, and the dirt-covered men eyed the gesture with puzzled expressions. "You guys don't shake hands in the future?"

Trexler shrugged uncomfortably, and Bobby dropped his arm.

"You might be right about that comet, who knows, and we don't see many people from your time. I'd imagine a lot of your customs are foreign to us. You see, we spend most of our lives hiding from and combating the boogeyman,"

"I can see," Bobby said.

As they headed out over the sea, the shoreline became more distant, and even the largest of the demons seemed small from their vantage point. Bobby felt an involuntary shudder as he thought of how close they had come to being eaten or crushed under the bootheels of terrifying monsters.

"They're not demons, you know. Not in the traditional *biblical* sense, anyway. The things out there breed, bleed, live, and die. Just like us, but they're often a lot bigger. And they live much longer if you don't kill 'em first," Dex said. It came out as a half-chuckle.

"You ever kill one?" Bobby asked.

"Oh sure, the cannons aboard the *Deezil* can take down almost any of them, even the winged rascals," Trexler said.

"Haven't seen one of those big guys in a long time, though," Dex said.

"What do the winged monsters look like?" Bobby asked.

"Best I can describe 'em is like big old dragons. We weren't sure what to call them until I ran across a book called *Puff the Magic Dragon* some years back. That one was friendly; these ain't. That's the difference. Big, scary mothers, too," Trexler said.

"Yeah, they'll eat your lunch. For sure," Dex said, shaking his head.

"Want to go out and get a better ocean view?" Dex asked.

"Is something going to swoop out of the clouds and try to eat us?" Bobby asked. "Most likely but living your life in fear ain't no life. Dex, give him a gun," Trexler said.

Dex reached into a small tool chest and produced a .38 snub-nose revolver that was so old that the black tape wrapped around it to keep the handle from falling apart was dry-rotted and cracking. The smaller man turned to Bobby and held the gun out, barrel down.

"Best I can do on short notice. Take it or leave it, kid," Dex said, tilting his head and nodding.

"No offense, but that thing might blow up in my hands. I'll use my sword; thank you, though," Bobby said.

"What sword?" Trexler said.

Bobby reached over his head to a small pocket in the top of his bag and brought out the handle of Ramos's weapon.

"Nice, you've got a sword hilt; you'd be better off taking the gun ki..." Trexler said.

His eyes went wide when Bobby squeezed the handle, and a two-and-a-half-inch-wide, three-foot- long blade of fire shot out of the slit in the stem.

"Wow!" Trexler said.

"Impressive. It looks like it's breathing," Dex said, mesmerized by the flame.

"Hey, kid! Put that thing away. Are you trying to blow us out of the sky?" Jasmine said.

"Crap! Sorry, Jasmine. Bobby, we're on a flying bomb," Dex said. Bobby apologized to Jasmine with a red face. "Let's go outside and get a better view. Come on, Bobby," Trexler said.

The teen replaced his hilt in the backpack, brushing his hand against the tablet. He blinked as the power surged through him for a second. As he followed the two crew members up a ladder, he felt his muscles twitch involuntarily, and when his hand wrapped around the safety rail, he bent the chrome rail. Bobby looked around to see if anyone else had seen him, but his father had already turned back to Jasmine, and the two were deep in conversation.

Serena was reading a tattered book she found on one of the chairs; Dante was slumped in a plush chair sleeping, and Ramos had the hood of his robe up, staring away, deep in thought. Bobby felt his muscles twitch again and pulled the rail back out, fixing the damage. This time, Serena caught a glimpse of what he was doing and raised her brow. When her brother vanished through the roof hatch, she ran her hand across the shiny steel rail, looking up where Bobby had been a moment ago. The only evidence of his damage was a tiny crimp in the metal.

"Nice trick, bro," Serena said to herself. She smiled and sat down again with her book. "I need to get my hands on that tablet." A few moments later, Bobby and his two new friends walked on the roof, looking out over the blue-green ocean.

"What is this craft? The *Deezil*, I mean. How'd you build it?" Mac asked.

"And where are we going?" Lilith asked.

"Long story about the *Deezil*, and we're headed to Pirate Island. One of the only places those forsaken towers weren't erected," Jasmine replied.

"How long a journey is it?" Lilith asked.

"About a day's flight. You're lucky we found you before those abominations did. Dex's energy anomaly detector picked you up when you used that device to return from the other planet.

"An energy anomaly detector?" Lilith asked. "Yeah, the EAD. We use it to find out whee portals are opening so we can go fry the suckers as they come in and out of them," Jasmine said.

"It was good you were nearby, but how were we that lucky?" Mac asked.

"We were returning from a supply run to old Wisconsin, one of the last working depots when we picked you up. Your friend's use of the purple fire in those woods was sheer stupidity, but it put a beacon on you; we almost had to ditch ya'll after you alerted every demon in the local area to your presence,"

"Ramos hasn't been himself lately, and I think it has something to do with the negative vibration here on Earth. I felt it as soon as we stepped over from the other side. What about the EAD?" Mac asked.

"Dex—our resident electronics genius and tinkerer—pieced it with some old computer parts we found in an underground bunker. When one of the towers is activated, a little green blip appears on an onscreen map, and we follow it there. But we also try to get to any unusually high energy signals if we can,"

"And we showed up on that device when you returned from your run," Mac said.

"Right, but ya'll were the highest register we've seen in more than twenty years of locating entry points," The voice came from a man walking back from the front of the train car.

The stranger came into view, and as soon as Lilith saw him, her eyebrows raised, and Mac detected a tiny smile. The man was six feet tall, muscular but not bulky, thirtyish, and sported a Mohawk haircut. The shaved sides of his head were inked with black tribal tattoos. The man wore jade piercings on his left and right ears, a skull earring through his right nostril, and goggles with telescoping lenses. His beard was short and dark, giving him the extra-added image of someone you do not want to mess with, Mac thought. He wore a T-shirt with cut-off sleeves that had at one point been black but was now gray, with a faded Batman symbol in the center. "That's true. We almost freaked out. An energy signature that size could mean a mass migration of monsters through the portal," Jasmine said.

"Name's Dominic. I'm the pilot, and Jasmine's my wife, er, better half anyway. So, you're a wolfman, huh? Never seen one of them come out of the portals," Dominic said.

"No, I'm still a human, just a little altered. It's a long story, but we left Earth in the year twenty-six. What year is it now?" Mac asked.

"It's close to twenty-two-ten, we think," Dominic said.

"Right, so we left around a hundred and fifty years ago to find a new home for mankind, but the people funding our mission were not exactly altruistic. Anyway, there was an incident on the planet Eritria where I almost died. I was dead for a few minutes, but after a blood transfusion, I mutated into a hybrid of their race. Look, it's going to sound crazy, but we came back to save the world,"

"He's telling the truth, apparently," Jasmine said and handed him the book with Mac's picture in it. "Alright, good enough for me. So how are we doing this save the world thing?" Dominic said.

"We have to get to Egypt. It involves the tablet my son carries in his backpack, the Ark of the Covenant, and the Great Pyramid. We have to get the tablet inside the pyramid with the Ark and then, I don't know, that's where the vision ended. "Alrighty then, that's a pretty crazy story, but then you see what we must live with daily. Who are the others in your crew?" Dominic asked.

Dominic reminded Mac of a man he served with in the Air Force during his basic training days. Spencer, something, Mac thought. He was brash, curt, and a brawler from the streets of Philadelphia who had been in so much trouble with the law that he was forced to choose between going into the military or spending six years in prison for a string of neighborhood crimes. The judge had taken pity on him because his parents were killed in a misdirected drive-by shooting. The shooter hit the wrong house and killed his parents during the evening news when Spencer was seven. His father was caught in the chest by three rounds, and two of them tore into his mother's forehead, killing her instantly. Mac remembered Spencer telling him that when the police and paramedics arrived, he was covered in her blood and trying to open her eyes.

"Dude, are you there?" Dominic asked. "Yeah, sorry, spaced out a bit," Mac said.

He told them about Dante, Ramos, Lilith, and their harrowing adventures on Eritria. When he was finished, their eyes were like saucers.

"Mac, that's the craziest crap I've ever heard. You folks got steel cojones surviving that mess. Welcome aboard the *Deezil*; you're officially part of the crew," Jasmine said. "Yeah, holy crap, that's like legendary man," Dominic said and reached up to clap a hand on Mac's shoulder.

"Thanks. But can this airship get us there?" Mac asked.

"I'm sorry to say no. The storms at sea are far too erratic and violent. While the armored balloon can deflect bullets, lightning is another story," Dominic said.

"You get freak lightning storms?" Mac asked. "Yeah, they come out of nowhere and have been ever since I can remember. You get them a lot back in the day?" Jasmine asked.

"They started around twenty-fifty-eight when the planet went out of balance, and our weather became extreme," Mac said.

"I know of a way we might be able to get you where you need to go," Jasmine said.

"No! I know what you're thinking, Jasmine, and I'm not dealing with those weird little beasts, again, not after last time," Dominic said.

"You got drunk and insulted their king, if I remember correctly. They had every right to throw you in jail," Jasmine said. She rolled her eyes and looked over at Mac.

"We're going to have to go to the faerie kingdom. They know of other portals within the Earth where you can travel between continents," Jasmine said. "They're dangerous, and they play tricks on humans. All I'll say about it," Dominic said. He was walking back to the front of the ship where the controls were.

"It'll be fine. Just mind your manners," Jasmine said.

"It's a bad idea!" Dominic said over his shoulder.

His voice was distant, almost comical to Mac.

"Did you say faeries?" Dante asked. He had woken up at the mention.

"We went to war with the faeries on my planet long ago," Ramos said.

"I don't know how they are where you come from, but they're nothing to mess with here, and they are easily offended," Jasmine said.

"The faerie war almost destroyed our people, and the aftermath separated the wolven into five tribes," Dante said.

"You could say we didn't get along very well," Ramos added.

"Jasmine, we're coming up on the island now! Home sweet home!" Dominic said he was yelling from the front.

"Please don't get us into any altercations with the faerie queen. We do not quarrel with her yet," Jasmine said.

Jasmine walked to the front, and the boys followed her. The train car was retrofitted with the front end of an engine car, and its windshield was in impressively good shape for its age.

"This is a pretty nice airship. Impressive engineering," Mac said.

He was looking out the windshield at an island in the middle of a fog bank, surrounded by crashing waves. In the center of the island was a giant stone castle with a massive wall surrounding it. The stones were thick and gray, and the towers tall and robust, a standing testament to the architectural prowess of an age long gone.

"I designed her myself and built the *Deezil* with the help of Dex and Trexler. That was about two years before we found Dominic fighting out of a burned-out city. You all want a tour of her before we land?" Jasmine asked.

"Lead the way," Dante said.

Jasmine nodded and turned to her left, opening a metal door. The door was attached to a room that made up a small hallway separating the pilot deck from the back of the long train car.

"This is the toilet room and shower, but the shower portion only works when it's raining," Jasmine said.

She opened the door to reveal a steel toilet bolted to the floor. When Mac went in to look through the bowl, he saw the ocean far below them and felt a breeze rushing up through the opening. Mac looked right and saw that the shower was a funnel attached to a showerhead connected to the ceiling. The floor was a steel grate with holes that had been pounded down in the center so that it modeled a drain. Two levers on the wall operated the device.

"Go ahead, try it out," Jasmine said.

Mac stooped down and entered the small room, careful not to bump his head on the doorframe. The room smelled like the ocean below, salty, but there was an industrial odor, like metal and petroleum. Mac held one lever and pulled it down, watching two doors below the large grate open down, and the other lever opened a hatch in the ceiling, which would allow the rainwater to pass through into the funnel above the shower taker's head in a passive drain. They had also fitted the shower wall with a soapbox, and inside was a small white bar of soap that smelled like lavender.

"Nice shower," Mac said.

"Thanks, moving on," Jasmine said. Each party member looked inside and nodded before following Jasmine down the hall.

Meanwhile, on top of the *Deezil*, Bobby was getting to know his new friends, Dex and Trexler. They were sitting on the ship's edge in Adirondack chairs behind a guardrail installed on the side that went all the way around the top of the train car. The black balloon floated peacefully above their heads, and as Bobby looked up, he noticed that the black fabric was a covering of some type. It looked like glued-on aluminum foil but thinner.

"What's the balloon covered with? That some funky aluminum foil?" Bobby asked.

"Nah, this is something the captain ran across when we were scrounging for supplies. That black covering can withstand a direct hit from a bullet and has protected us during a few nasty dogfights with some dragons," Trexler said.

"Where'd she find it?" Bobby asked.

"There was this tunnel in the woods, and it must have been a pretty important place at one time because beside it, hanging on busted hinges, was a two-foot-thick steel and cement-reinforced door. The trees had overgrown the whole area, and we almost missed it, but Jasmine spotted the opening by chance," Dex said.

"Yeah, and neither of us wanted to venture inside. That tunnel was dark and deep, and places like that in this world are great hiding spots for bears, demons, dog packs, and so on," Trexler said.

"So anyway, Jasmine takes out her lantern and just walks in," Dex said.

"Of course, we followed her; we ain't punks," Trexler said.

"Yeah," Dex said.

"Well, she gets to the back of this tunnel, and an elevator still functions. We figure it must have gotten its power from underground generators or solar energy, but we never found the source. Anyway, it must have been some government facility because they had all kinds of cool things like the black sheeting that covers this balloon," Trexler said.

"And the computer parts I needed to craft the energy anomaly detector. It works off GPS, too. Did you know those satellites still function in space after all this time?" Dex said.

"That's how you found us so fast, right?" Bobby asked.

"We couldn't find your exact location, but we can triangulate energy distortions within half a mile of their origination. Your fire was what led us to you," Dex said.

"Yeah, talk about a beacon! You had every monster and demon within ten miles headed your way," Trexler said.

"What are you boys talking about up here? I heard 'monsters and demons.'" Jasmine asked. Mac and the rest of the party were behind her, save for Serena, who was below deck sleeping on the couch. "We were telling him about the tunnel you found this bulletproof covering in," Dex said.

"That's not all we found either; the engines that power our jet thrusters were also down there. I looked through some folders and stacks of books and found out that the people who used to work there had created quantum energy generators. After playing with them, I discovered they can produce unlimited energy from a set of magnetic rings inside. I fitted them to some old airplane turbines I discovered in an aircraft graveyard, and boom! Thruster engines without the need for fuel," Jasmine said.

The *Deezil* was coming in for a landing on top of the castle keep.

"Looks like we're here. Everybody off the ship, let's eat," Jasmine said.

CHAPTER 7

THE DEEZIL TOUCHED DOWN ATOP the castle keep as a bank of thick fog rolled in across the ocean, bringing fresh salty air. The ship's crew and her adventurous new passengers stepped off into relative safety for the first time in an extraordinarily long time. Mac looked around at the castle's architecture and felt as if he were hundreds of years in the past when King Arthur and his knights of the Round Table were searching for the Holy Grail. Waves crashed beyond the castle barrier walls, sweeping over giant rocks that made up the coastline.

"This was never a vacation spot for the casual sunbather," Mac said.

He walked to the keep wall and looked over to see a moat spanning the gap between the castle and its exterior walls. Large snakelike bodies writhed over each other in the broad waterless expanse, gnashing at each other, disappearing into tunnels cut beneath the structure.

"I guess it'd be a bad day for anyone falling into that," Mac said.

"Those are the eels, genetically modified to exist on land. They have tiny feet under those bodies but can't run fast. Just don't fall into their pit, or it's lights out," Jasmine said.

"Who modified them?" Bobby asked.

"We don't know...exactly. All my research points to clandestine laboratories in places like former Atlanta, Georgia. A center there worked on infectious diseases and all kinds of gene splicing," Trexler said.

"Humans created these creatures?" Mac asked. "The very first creations were manmade, but oven time, they evolved into what you see down there," Jasmine said.

"I've seen the sharks on your planet, and their sheer size is...unnatural. The creatures on Earth were much different thousands of years ago," Lilith said.

"Just how old are you, lady?" Dominic asked.

Jasmine cut her eyes at him and back at Lilith. "That's a good question," Jasmine said.

Lilith sighed and looked first at Mac and then to the others. "I'm older than you can imagine. I'm part of a long-lost bloodline of scientists and engineers who travel the universe searching for life and minerals." "Wait a minute; you don't mean to say you're the Lilith from the Sumerian records?" Trexler asked.

"It's more complicated than that, but that's me," Lilith said.

"The demon, Lilith, she who comes in the night to seduce men?" Dex asked.

Lilith rolled her eyes. "I was promised to Adamu, in your scripture Adam, and when I refused to submit to him, the people who created me gave him another concubine. Her name was Eve, and my name was maligned and associated with evil deeds, but I never did anything to deserve the title of demon or succubus. Men and their twisted agendas have caused more problems for women over time than all the plagues in the world."

"So, how did you get to Eritria?" Mac asked. "I stowed away on a ship leaving Earth during the last major cataclysm, and I escaped from them when we landed on Eritria,"

"You are full of mysteries, my friend," Mac said. He walked over and gave her a bear hug, lifting her off the ground.

"Thanks, big guy. Now, let me down before I set you on fire," Lilith said. She kissed him on the mouth. "We have to do something about that dog breath," She waved her hand in front of her nose. "You're ripe."

"Hey, we have great breath!" Dante said. He chuffed a breath into his hand, sniffed the air and wrinkled his nose. "OK, it's good, not great." For the first time in weeks, Mac felt the steel band wrapped around his chest loosen a bit. He felt a lighthearted calm drift over them like an invisible mist.

"Inside, food, let's go," Jasmine said.

"Who's the chef tonight?" Dominic asked. "Trexler, you're up. I cooked last night," Dex said.

"I hope you like eel and beans 'cause that's what's getting made," Trexler said.

"I'm starving," Ramos said. His eyes had a purple tint, and he had been quiet most of the day.

"Brother, you are doing alright?" Dante asked.

His brow furrowed with concern.

"I'm as fine as I can be," Ramos said. The purple faded as he turned to Dante, but the younger wolven wasn't buying it.

"Sure, sure, you look fine to me. Well, eel sounds great. I'll eat whatever you throw in front of me. I ain't fussy," Dante said, and Ramos nodded.

The party followed Jasmine to a doorway leading down into the castle, but before Lilith descended, she turned back to see the figure they had encountered in the corpse monster pit.

"Azrael," she said.

"Lilith, so good to see you again," Azrael said. He was grinning and ogling her body through gray, flinty eyes.

"That was four thousand years ago, and my feelings for you are no fonder now than they were then. This is no longer your realm, demon. The Anunnaki claimed Earth and the planets of this solar system long ago," Lilith said.

"Perhaps their slaves should not have tampered with temporal distortions then. We have as much of a right to this world as they do. In fact, during the last cataclysm, they got inside their little spaceships and departed to parts unknown," Azrael said.

"We will not allow you to destroy this planet. You have your home world, to which you will return or face the wrath," Lilith said.

"I'm not going to stand here and debate anything with you, hag. I think my master would very much like to have Colonel MacDonald as a pet, I mean, guest, in his castle," Azrael said.

"Why, what possible reason could Lucifer have for wanting Mac?" Lilith said.

"He and his kind are heroes! Their meddling in the quantum field allowed us to cross over," Azrael said. He flexed his long bat-like wings and grinned wickedly.

"What are you talking about?" Lilith said.

"Had the Colonel and his merry band of idiots never constructed the Tesla towers, Earth's weather anomalies would have reset the planet, and in a hundred years or so, humanity would have been right back on track," Azrael said.

"You're lying; he knew nothing about the towers, and even if he did, how would he know about the weather? Lilith asked.

"Why don't you ask him? In the end, in their desperation, the human military set those towers up to help save themselves—without any knowledge of how they work," Azrael said. He laughed.

"We're kicking you out as soon as we get where we're going. Don't get too comfortable, Azrael," Lilith said.

"Oh, I don't think so; you'll be dead!" Azrael said. A loud bang rang out in the air, and Azrael stopped talking mid-sentence as a black circle opened on his forehead. His eyes rolled back, and he fell over like a statue to the hard stone of the floor. Lilith turned around and saw Mac with his rifle raised, one eye fixed on the sights, his finger on the trigger. When she fixed her gaze on him, he grinner and dropped the gun to his side. "Somebody had to shut that guy up," Mac said. "Thanks," Lilith said.

"I heard something about us being dead, and that's where I draw the line. A friend of yours?" Mac asked.

"Right hand of the Devil. Hey, what did he mean when he said you knew about the Tesla towers and the weather returning to normal?" Lilith said.

"What?" Mac said.

Dante and Ramos returned to see what was happening and saw the winged demon lying flat on his back.

"I just didn't think it was worth mentioning?" Dante asked.

"You hid the truth from me, Mac," Lilith said. "Hid is a strong word, Lilith. I was trying to forget the past," Mac said.

"You were trying to forget your guilt," she quipped.

"Yes, that's true."

"Why would you hide this from us?"

Mac balled his fists. "Did I know they were being built? Yes. Did we know the world would return to normal in around a hundred years? Yes, we knew, but there was never any mention of interdimensional portals in the tower plans. That was a miscalculation, but the alternative was to allow the world population to decrease to around five hundred thousand people."

"If that is the way things are, then it should have been allowed to take place without interference," Lilith said.

"Famine, disease, war, pestilence? We should have done nothing at all to prevent that?"

"Yes, in my time alive I have seen many societies rise and fall under their own technology, but never have I seen one rip the fabric of space and time to save themselves," Lilith said.

"Then you don't know humans," Mac replied. Jasmine stood beside Ramos. "Yeah, we'll do whatever we have to for survival."

"In your desire to survive extinction, you caused an even worse turn of events," Lilith said.

"If you're saying this is *my* fault..." Mac said. "No, not at all, but for all of our sake, I hopd you're right about the Tablet of Destinies because these guys are not going away without some encouragement," Lilith said.

"I'm guessing there will be more of them on their way, seeing as Mac has just killed one of their elites," Ramos said.

"Mac, toss that corpse over the side for the eels, and let's go eat," Dante said. "The dead of this world whisper in my mind, and tell me someone named Baal is coming," Ramos said.

"Tall, dark, and stormy has spoken. I'm heading down to get some food before another fight breaks out. It simply never ends," Dante said, walking through the doorway leading down.

Mac and Lilith dropped the body over the wall, and it vanished under the pile of writhing eel bodies. As the demon lord's right-hand commander rolled under the biting, chewing mouths of the eels, Mac had a sinking feeling that Ragnok, Asura, and Broad Axe may have been a training ground compared to the armies of Hell. For the first time since returning through the cosmic portal, he regretted coming back. "Don't give up just yet, my dear," Lilith said. She stroked the back of his neck gently.

"You read minds as well, now?" Mac asked. "No, it's written on your face. Believe me when e say that as long as I've lived, I have seen far worse than the predicament you and your people are in," Lilith said.

"I just never thought it would be this bad. Never even considered the possibility that the humans fighting in the streets would be replaced with monsters from another world," Mac said. "Right, but we have the spirits of the warrior gods on our side and will prevail," Lilith said. They looked out at the ocean and the foggy wall surrounding the castle. Mac touched Lilith's as they leaned against the three-foot-tall stone wall.

"If the faeries can help, they will. But be careful not to fall under the spell of their queen, or you'll never leave their kingdom," Lilith said.

"Lilith, I wouldn't worry about that. I've got a strong constitution," Mac said.

"Haha, that's got nothing to do with it, Mac. Just know that where we're going is dangerous ground. If they get you into a faerie circle, there's nothing we can do to get you out, and you won't want us to either."

"I'll have to keep a close eye on Bobby as well, I guess," Mac said.

"Not a bad idea," Lilith said. She led Mac to the doorway, and they descended into the ancient castle to join their friends for dinner.

Mac and Lilith entered a grand ballroom where in the center sat a long wooden table where the Deezil and their party crew were seated, talking, and eating. Trexler had just finished cooking the eel, and as Mac sat at the table, he watched with distrust as steam rose from the blackened beast. Trexler, the excellent host, cut large pieces off and passed it around the table.

"They don't look like they'd be good eating when you first see them, but eels are delicious," Trexler said.

"Especially with the spices Trexler uses," Dex said.

"Yeah, that's why we always rope him into cooking. None of you other jerks can cook for crap," Jasmine said. Laughter rang out around the table from the crew as they nodded. Trexler gave them an indignant headshake.

"Laugh it up, but she's right. You better hope I stay alive, or you'll all starve to death," Trexler said. "What was that noise coming from the roof?" Dominic asked Lilith and Mac.

"Azrael, one of the high lieutenants in Lucifer's army, popped in to threaten us, and when he did, Mac shot him in the head," Lilith said. She leaned over and kissed Mac on his muzzle, and he grinned. "Great, so much for a haven in the ocean; they'll hunt us here now. The demons will come for his body," Dex said. His head was in his hands, and he was pulling at the bangs of dark, matted hair witl his dirt-smudged fingers. "Just what we needed. Now we're in hock with the devil," Dominic said. He pounded a fist on the table.

"Hey, look. I saw a shot and took it. He was talking about killing all of us anyway, and from my experiences lately, you kill your enemy while you've got the opportunity, no quarter given. Our old guard used to call it a preemptive strike," Mac said.

"Yeah, and look at how that turned out for them. Maybe if the *old guard* hadn't had that mentality, the world would be far different," Dex said.

"You've got a point," Mac said.

"And that's right when everything went to crap, wasn't it?" Dex said.

"Boys, calm down," Lilith said.

"Where's the body? You didn't leave it on the roof, did you?" Dex asked.

"Nope, we tossed it over the side and let the eels have him, so there's no body left to claim," Mac said. "Great, now our food supply is contaminated!"

Trexler said.

"Hey, listen, I'm sorry, guys. It was a reflex action," Mac said.

"That means Baal won't be far behind," Jasmine said.

"You've met the demon lords before?" Lilith asked. "I was captured by a demon and taken to a dark castle inside that strange gray world across the portals. If it hadn't been for Dominic, I never would have escaped. Baal was one of my interrogators, and as Azrael's twin, what one feels, the other reciprocates, and they could see through each other's eyes," Jasmine said.

"You say we're dealing with Lucifer, so that world through the Tesla portals is Hell?" Mac asked. "You might call it Hell or chaotic evil," Jasminh said.

"How do you know it's Hell?" Bobby said. "While I was being tortured, Baal's mine connected with mine for a moment, and I saw an ocean of the damned burning in a lake of fire. They were screaming and writhing in this fiery chasm. You know, the people, souls, whatever were never consumed by the flames, just immersed in them. Winged creatures fly around the lake perpetually, dropping more people into the lake," Jasmine said. A tear fell from her good eye.

"I knew where they had taken her, so I flew the *Deezil* into one of those portals, and while the boys here watched my back, I landed her on top of the castle and ran inside. But I'm sad my rescue attempt was a little late," Dominic said. "That's where I got this," Jasmine said, pointing to the eye patch. "Baal took my eye with a metal claw hook,"

"Yeah, so if he was torturing you for fun while his brother was alive, just imagine his reaction to finding out Azrael's dead," Dex said.

"We'll have to clear out before dawn if we have that long," Trexler said.

"These demons are at least mortal, and if they can bleed, they can die, and we stand a chance," Mac said.

"Daddy, you should give me a gun. Just in case," Serena said. Mac considered his teenage daughter for a minute and realized she might have a point.

"OK, you can have mine," Mac said. He passed his rifle to her and began to eat.

The conversation dropped until everyone had eaten their fill, and then Jasmine handed out orders to supply the *Deezil* with rations and weapons. As they were loading the airship, Mac caught up to Jasmine on the keep's roof and pulled her aside.

"I genuinely hope I have not caused more damage than good, Jasmine. I honestly thought I was helping," Mac said.

"Look, we've been at war with these evil things since the day those portals were opened. One more of them dead is not a bad thing, Mac. Don't sweat it; you and your team are the first light we've seen in many years. The last of the rebellions were put down over seventy-five years ago," Jasmine said.

"Well, that makes me feel a little better," Mac said.

"I've found methods that help me survive the insanity, and one of them is this: never apologize for doing the right thing, no matter how much it might seem like it sucks," Jasmine said. She patted Mac on the chest, just above his heart. "Go with what's in here," Then she gave him a friendly smile and tended to a crate of supplies. Mac joined her and lifted a munitions container with *Aerial Mine* stenciled on the front. It sat atop another wooden box marked *Rocket Launcher* with black spray paint stenciled letters.

"These weapons have to be older than me. Are you sure they're safe?" Mac said. Jasmine chuckled. "Well, if they aren't, we won't have much to worry about for long. With as much boom boom as we have on this rig, we'll all be blown to tiny pieces," Jasmine said.

"Comforting," Mac said.

"Relax, Colonel, we haven't had an accident yet with the remaining weapons of the old world. Besides, we found them in an airtight underground bunker," Jasmine said. "You find anything else?" Mac asked. "Some tanks and other vehicles."

"Were any of them still running?" Mac asked. "The fuel was all dead, you know, flat, and none of them ran on quantum drives, so we took what we could use and left the rest behind," Jasmine said.

Darkness settled in as night approached, and a thicker bank of fog reduced visibility to zero. Mac felt nervous as he stood in the open with Jasmine, unable to see more than two feet before him.

"What's with the fog? It is ever-present here on your little island," Mac asked.

"The fog's a natural veil of protection. There's dry land two miles to the east, where the ancestors raised three Tesla towers, but thanks to the fog, our hideout has been a sanctuary from the beasts,"

There was a faint buzzing in the distance, like the sound of a lawnmower.

"Crap!" Trexler yelled. He ran out of the *Deezil* like a rabid dog was chasing him. "Get inside. Now! Locusts!" He spoke.

Dex was not far behind him, but his expression was a mixture of fear and confusion as he looked at Jasmine and Mac standing outside.

"Get inside!" Trexler said. His voice faded as he ran through the door and down the staircase. "I'd listen to him!" Dex said. He was gone in a flash through the door and shut it behind him.

The first locusts slapped like rain against the *Deezil's* balloon as Mac and Jasmine looked at each other. In the next instant, they ran for cover as winged pests thumped their backs like pellets from a rifle. Jasmine tossed the door open and tripped through the doorway, her face covered in a mask of obnoxious insects. Mac remained as calm as he could and nudged her with his foot while he entered and shut the door behind them. Mac could feel them crawling inside his fur, burrowing through matted tangles of dirty, salty hair, and he clawed at his flesh, crushing hundreds of them into green goo.

"Get them off of me!" Jasmine screamed.

Mac calmed his revulsion and put away the discomfort of the stinging locusts to help Jasmine out. He scooped two handfuls of them from her face and tossed them to the floor, crushing the mass under his massive feet. Trexler was there a moment later, helping his captain.

"I'm so sorry, Cap. I saw em' a split second too late," Trexler said.

He cleared some more insects off her as she regained her composure and sat with her back against the wall, breathing heavily. Mac managed to stomp most of them into green slime on the floor and began to clear his fur of the biting nuisance. He slammed himself into the wall a few times, crushing the remaining creepy crawlies under his coat, and then sat down next to Jasmine, who was picking bodies off her clothes.

"That was messed up," Mac said.

They could hear locust bodies plinking into the door like hail.

"This is actually what I expected," Jasmine said. "What?" Mac asked.

"We're at war with an unholy army, Mac, and the creepy crawlies are their emissaries. This is the first retaliation for Azrael," Jasmine said. She was shaking her head slowly as she leaned against the wall, her face welted and swelling from bites.

"We came here to take this planet back, and we're going to do just that," Mac said.

"That's the right attitude, Colonel! Baal will be along soon enough and trust me when I say we don't want to fight him yet. The locusts are the first plague," Jasmine said.

"Plagues are coming?" Mac asked.

"I've never seen one, but my great-grandmother used to talk about the wars her parents fought with the monsters when she was tiny, back when there were more people. The plagues would hit 'em first, weaken their defenses, and then the demons would come after that," Trexler said.

"How many plagues are we talking about?" Mac said.

"Grasshoppers, locusts, frogs, mosquitoes, but it doesn't matter if you're right about the pyramid because we'll finally be able to stop them. I was planning to bug out at first light, but we're going to have to move that up a bit and take off tonight," Jasmine said. Dominic was rounding the corner and running up the stairs with everyone else behind him. "What's going on? Bugs are pounding the castle.

They're everywhere down there," Dominic said. "Baal is coming, and we need to leave," Jasmind said.

"And miss a fight? We haven't had one of those in at least a day. Why leave now?" Dante asked, standing in the stairwell with his brother.

"Because we're pinned down on this little island, and the mouth of Hell is opening up to swallow us," Jasmine said.

"Makes sense," Ramos said.

"But, if you want to charge out there and do battle all by yourself, you're more than welcome, Dante," Jasmine said. An ominous roar shook the castle, and each of them exchanged glances as the sound of locusts stopped abruptly.

"I think our time here is growing short," Ramos said. The fight has come." His eyes glowed purple once more, and he stepped around people on the stairwell to get to the door.

"Don't open that door. We have no idea what's on the other side," Dex said.

"This is foolishness; we've got to hide in the tunnels until the monsters are gone," Trexler said. "We don't hide," Dante said and followed his brother.

"They're right. We've got a mission to carry out, and not even Hell will stop us," Mac said.

Ramos tossed the door open and stepped out into a fog of flying locusts. Dex hit the light switch on the wall next to the door, and a floodlight illuminated the keep court. There was a bright glare as if the sun had risen over the distant horizon, burning through the fog, giving them visibility. Jasmine stood up, brushing herself off.

"Let's get out there and back them up!" Dex said and pointed to the figures of skeletal soldiers climbing over the walls.

Ramos shot a stream of purple flames from his hands, burning through the locust swarm, turning them to cinders and small, black lumps of charcoal. Another swarm of the winged pests surrounded the *Deezil* as the first of the skeletal soldiers put a rattling, booted foot on the stone floor. Ramos set fire to every living thing in his path, ensuring not to hit the *Deezil*.

"Get on the *Deezil* and get her airborne, Dominic!" Jasmine said.

"I'm on it!" Dominic said, "Dex, you're coming with me!" The duo ran to the airship and boarded her, kicking off locusts.

"Do it before Ramos sets all our equipment on fire!" Jasmine said.

Dante ran to the right wall and saw ladders leaning against them from across the mote, with skeletons, dog-faced mid-sized demons, and imps crossing the ladders as if they were bridges. A few devils tossed fireballs into the mote of eels below, roasting the slippery, slimy quadruped creatures. They would be across soon, so Dante decided to slow them down.

"Hey, boys! Don't look down," Dante said.

He slid the ladder to the left and watched as it vanished into the pit of eels below. Imp screams rose over the rattling of bones as the eels consumed them and their skeletal friends, bone, and all. But soon, more ladders crossed the chasm, and more enemies came.

"Cap'n, you want me to set off the birthday cake?" Trexler asked Jasmine.

She was reaching for her gun and saber, leaving the relative safety of the stone stairwell, when he came up from behind. She turned to look at him with trepidation.

"How long's it take to go off?" Jasmine asked. "We calculated it at about five minutes. It should be enough time if Dex and Dominic get the *Deezil* airborne," Trexler said.

She sighed, taking one last look around her castle. "Do it, but get your ass back up here, we're leaving in three," Jasmine said.

She ran into the fray of ferocious undead soldiers and oncoming imps, armed with a plasma pistol and a proper sky pirate's sword.

"AAAAAARRRRGHHHH!" Jasmine said. Her war face brought a new level of energy to the fight. Dante pushed all of the demons he could get to over the wall while Ramos summoned spirits of the damned to possess their bodies.

"This should slow them down!" Ramos said, muttering under his breath.

He willed them to throw each other over the sides of the walls and even set some of them against one another in hand-to-hand combat. The Deezil lifted off as the army began to fight itself.

"Get aboard the ship! Everyone...now!" Jasmine said.

Jasmine ran to the castle door to usher Bobby and Serena to the ship. Lilith had been flying above them all, fighting a dragon with massive wings and fire for breath in the sky. She was throwing balls of orange flame at the beast, diving out of the way as it attempted to roast her, keeping Lilith trapped in a stalemate as time ticked down on the castle bomb. Bobby ran with his sister, and in minutes, almost all of them were onboard, except Lilith.

"I got a good shot if she gets out of the way!" Dex said. He was looking into an eyepiece with the barrel of an old tank cannon pointed at Lilith and her attacker.

"Lilith, drop down!" Mac said. She turned back, nodded, and let her wings fold in a bit.

She fell out of view, and Dex pushed a button on a board before him at the front of the *Deezil*. Dex saw what looked like a half-man, half-dragon appear in his eyepiece, and then the thunder of his round pierced the night. Whatever it was vanished in a cloud of smoke and blood spray. Lilith joined them on the airship a few moments later, which was now hovering off the ground. "Thanks for the hand!" Lilith said.

Trexler came running across the keep waving his hands like a madman, and Bobby threw the chain ladder down for him.

"Go! Go! Go!" Trexler yelled. "The birthday cake's about to light up!"

Dominic threw a switch, and a sound like a generator winding up at the back of the *Deezil* made Mac's ears prick up. In the next instant, they were more than a mile away from the castle, just in time to watch a mushroom cloud replace the castle. Screams of agony and rage echoed through the night as the demons were blown violently apart in the explosion and were denied their revenge.

CHAPTER 8

JASMINE'S BLAZING CASTLE VANISHED IN the distance moments after Dex pressed a button on the central console, activating the *Deezil's* rear engines. In an instant, the makeshift airship whooshed through the night on silent thrusters powered by quantum energy and away from the deadly hordes. The engines carried them hundreds of miles away in minutes.

"That went better than I thought it would," Trexler said.

"What? Blowing up our home?" Dex asked. "Well, yeah. I wired that place with so many explosives that those monster mothers will be roasting in the fire until they're ashes," Trexler said. The castle was gone now, and they were soaring through the darkness as waves rolled below them over an endless sea. "You think they're chasing us?" Lilith asked. "Hard to say. Like I said before, crossing the ocean is too dangerous, and most demons prefer portal travel," Jasmine said.

As if in response to her statement, a lightning strike flashed through the darkness with the brilliance of a thousand suns, striking the ocean below.

"We've got to get to dry land before the lightning takes us down. This ain't gonna get any better," Trexler said.

"I know where we're going, but it's hard to find in the dark," Dominic said.

Jasmine's eyes widened, and she held up a finger. "Wait one minute," she said and dashed to the back of the *Deezil*. She returned a moment later, holding goggles resembling two small telescopee with a strap around the back.

"I found these in a storage compartment in that old underground bunker. I tried them on one day and found that I could see perfectly in the dark!" Jasmine said. She handed them to Dominic.

"You didn't think this information would be critical before now?" Dominic asked. He looked back at her with a smart-alecky grin and raised eyebrows. "You better be grinning. We never needed them before now since traveling at night is next to suicide," Jasmine said and shot a glance over at Mac and his compatriots.

"Looks like times are changing, my dear," Dominic said. He placed the goggles over his eyes.

"That's Captain to you," Jasmine said. Dominic kissed her on the cheek, and she shrugged him off.

"Wow! It's like daylight out there!" Dominic said. "I can see the island now."

He steered them toward the destination as two more bolts of lightning shot out of the blackness, narrowly missing their craft.

"Here we go, everyone!" Dominic said. They could feel the craft descending, and a lightning bolt shot directly through the *Deezil*.

They were instantly plummeting toward the ocean through the darkness of a black, moonless night. Bobby and Serena came running from the back of the craft with sleep in their eyes as the Amtrak car slammed hard into the water. Dex had been sitting next to Mac when the lightning struck, and as it hit, he put his hand on Dex's knee. The small Indian man fell sideways, and Serena began to scream. To Mac's surprise and horror, Dex no longer had a head. The lightning blew through the roof of the airship and cut Dex in half on its way to the water below.

"Everyone out!" Jasmine screamed. "Before the lightning strikes again!" She looked down at Dex's body floating in the salty ocean water. "You people are either a blessing or a lesson. Let's go, everyone off," Jasmine screamed.

"Lands about fifty yards that way," Dominic said. He was pointing and moving to the now-submerged porthole under their ship. "We're gonna have to swim for it. Watch out for sharks!"

Lilith ushered the children toward the porthole as Mac followed behind her. Ramos was already free of the sinking wreck, and Dante was waiting for Mac to go through before he dived in. Trexler held Dex in his arms for a moment and then dropped his lifeless body into the brine.

"Crap, there's blood in the water!" Trexler yelled. With that, a tentacle the thickness of a telephone pole busted through the *Deezil*'s window and snatched Trexler off his feet. It happened so fast that he didn't have time to scream before he was gone. Jasmine looked back in time to see a look of frozen shock on Trexler's face. Then, her historian, confidant, and friend was pulled away by an unsees horror of the deep. "This isn't happening! This isn't happening!" Serena screamed.

"Sweetie, it is, and you have to hold on to me.

Take my hand. I won't let go," Mac said.

"The monster is out there," Serena said. Bobby passed by and dived through the hole.

"Follow your brother, come on! You can do this," Mac said.

Something gripped the Deezil, and as Mac and Serena dived through the hole, the ship's hull began to rise out of the water. Bobby was treading water as his sister and father landed right beside him. Lilith exploded out of the shattered front window; she held Jasmine in her arms as her wings carried her up and away.

Dominic was struggling to get through the window, and there was a shard of glass sticking out of his ribs. The tentacle lifted the ship high into the air, with Dominic hanging out of the window, holding a bomb in his hand. Lilith set Jasmine down on the coastline and flew up to get Dominic. Her eyes were ablaze as she tossed fireballs at the tentacle. The monster attached to it rose out of the water, irritated, and injured by her attack. It was an enormous squid with a parrot's beak the size of a small building. As it opened its mouth, the tentacle shook Dominic out of the train car and into its gullet. With a final scream, Dominic disappeared.

"Nooooooo!" Jasmine shouted. "I got him!" Lilith said.

Lilith surged forward, and she was blown back toward the beach, tumbling through the air as chunks of gore splattered the turbulent ocean. A moment later, the others swam and reached the shore before three enormous sharks entered the bloodbath and battled over the squid's carcass in a fierce and violent feast. To Serena, who was now safely on dry land, the sharks looked like buses crashing into each other in the dark.

Jasmine had her head in her hands, repeating Dominic's name repeatedly. Her mind was in shock as Lilith landed next to her and sat down.

"Jasmine! Are you alright?" Lilith asked.

"I'm fine!" Jasmine said and pounded her fist into the white sand. "I did not see that coming."

When she looked up, tears were streaming down her face, and although Lilith wanted to feel sorry for her, it was not in her nature, and she wondered for a moment if she had been alive too long.

"I'm sorry about Dominic," Serena said and sat on the sand beside Jasmine.

"Trexler and Dex are gone as well. My whole family was on that ship," Jasmine said. "I'm sorry for your loss," Lilith said.

Lilith quickly touched Jasmine's shoulder and walked away to where Mac was pulling himself out of the ocean, dragging Dante behind him. The wolven warrior was unconscious.

"What's the matter with Dante? Is he OK?" Lilith asked.

"Yeah, fine, I think. He took a nasty blow to the head when that train car was lifted out of the water," Mac said.

Serena put an arm around Jasmine. "You've got us, Jasmine. We'll be your family now."

"Thanks, sweetie. I appreciate that." Jasmine put her arm around Serena.

Ramos walked over to Dante and knelt beside his brother's face.

"You in there?" Ramos said and thumped Dante on the nose.

The unconscious wolven sprang to his feet, claws out, panting. "Who did that?! What sick son of a wolven wants to die tonight?" Dante said.

"You'd be surprised how many times that has worked," Ramos said, turning to Mac. Ramos's hood was down, and he tapped his head. "Dante was born with a strong skull and a small brain,"

"You're a poet, brother," Dante said. "You alright?" Mac asked. "Fine, never been better," Dante fell over and passed out face up in the sand.

"That's not fine," Bobby said, walking up to them.

"He needs to sleep it off, but Dante will regenerate by morning. Fast healing is one of my people's traits,"

Bobby still wore his backpack. Mac grabbed the flap and saw that it was cinched shut.

"Yes, Dad, the tablet's safe," Bobby said. His tone was sarcastic.

"The only reason we left paradise was to bring that object back here, so maybe tone down the attitude?" Mac said.

"You're right, sorry, Dad," Bobby said. I'll take tall, dark, and furry here and set him under a tree to sleep." Before Mac could caution him, his son had hoisted the easily three-hundred-pound wolven man over his shoulder and was walking up the beach toward a palm tree. Mac and Ramos exchanged expressions of confused surprise.

"It seems your son may not be telling you something," Ramos said.

"I knew the tablet could affect him; you think that's it?" "Impressive strength," Ramos said. He clapped Mac on the shoulder, and they walked up to where Serena was sitting next to Jasmine.

"It's a senseless tragedy," Mac said.

"Yeah, well, everything looks better in the light of day and I'm tired of pretty much everything right now, so I'm gonna check out for a while," Jasmine said.

She had been wearing a flannel shirt, and although it was soaked from their crash landing in the ocean, she took it off, revealing a black sleeveless T-shirt. She piled up sand beneath it and rolled over on her side, away from the others. In minutes, her devastated mind shut down, and she drifted into a dreamless slumber.

"How are you doing, kiddo?" Mac asked Serena. "Not great, but Jasmine lost everyone she loven so that it could be worse. I want to get some sleep, too," Serena said.

She piled up sand into a mound and turned to face Jasmine's back. In the brief time she had known her, Jasmine was the closest thing she'd had to a mom since her mother passed away, and it was a relief to be around another human female she respected.

"Good night, sweetie," Mac said, kissing his daughter on the back of her head. "Night, Dad, see ya' in the morning," Serena said, falling fast asleep.

Lilith walked over to Ramos and Mac and caught Mac's eyes, glancing at Jasmine's shapely behind. She smirked but said nothing.

"You boy's going to sleep tonight?" Lilith asked. She walked with a swagger, and the sway of her hips instantly regained Mac's attention.

"In a few, I guess. I'm pretty wired from that crash," Mac said.

"I know how we can take care of that. But you've got to switch back to human form." Ramos grinned. "Heh heh, I'm going to go find my brother ans get some sleep myself," he said.

Bobby laid Dante under a palm tree, looked around to ensure no one was watching them, and withdrew the medical supply pack from his backpack. Mac had thrown it in as a precaution against disaster, containing a syringe and rubber tourniquet. Dante was out cold, and the closest person to them was over a hundred feet away, but he would have to act quickly or get caught. Bobby tied off Dante's arm, and when the vein in his arm was exposed, Bobby stuck the needle in and pulled back on the plunger.

"I hope you don't wake up, man," Bobby said.

He was nervous and breathing heavily. He could make out the outline of the dark fluid entering his blood delivery system with little light. As he finished drawing the blood he needed for his experiment, he saw the figure of Ramos coming his way, with those creepy purple glowing eyes. He would have to move fast, and the tourniquet was still around Dante's arm. He quickly undid the rubber strap and tied it around his arm until the circulation began to slow, and he felt a familiar tingle of numbness. It reminded him of how blood pressure cuffs would tighten on his arm until his fingers felt like a balloon.

"Do it now, or ditch this thing, Bobby," Bobby said, whispering to himself. He hesitated. "What if his blood kills me? What if it doesn't?" Bobby placed the tip of his syringe at the spot where he felt his primary vein rising, and with a deep breath, he stuck it in.

At first, he felt a slight pinch under the skin, and then, as he began to press the plunger down, liquid fire coursed through his veins like slow lava down the side of a volcano. Bobby's super strength allowed him to keep pushing on the plunger, but the pain was so intense that he curled into the fetal position and began to moan.

"Bobby?" Ramos asked.

Ramos created a light with purple fire from his hands, illuminating the boy with spectral brilliance. Ramos called his name again, but the young man did not respond, save for moans and grunts. He was writhing on the ground with a transparent tube- shaped object sticking out of his left arm at the crease in his elbow. Bobby flipped over, and Ramos could see that the boy had ripped his shirt apart in his distress, and it was lying in tatters on the sand. His skin looked like an army of bugs marching under the flesh, rippling like undulating waves on an ocean. Bobby gritted his teeth together while he screamed.

"Mac! Get over here; it's your son!" Ramos said. He levitated a purple fireball over the boy to give them light.

Mac ran over to where Ramos stood and knelt beside his flailing son. The moment he did, Bobby stopped moving and lay still in the sand, the needle having fallen out of his arm and onto the ground beside him.

"Bobby! Bobby!" Mac said. "Crap! Wake up, son," Mac looked at the syringe on the ground and held it to the purple light. "He's injected himself with something!"

He looked up, and Jasmine stood over him, concern creasing her brow. "What happened?"

"I don't know. You didn't happen to have any drugs onboard that craft, did you?" Mac asked. "We haven't had drugs outside of marijuana in over fifty years," Jasmine said.

Mac remembered the first aid kit he'd placed in Bobby's backpack and tried to remember if anything were there. He opened the bag, rooting around inside until he found the kit, but there was nothing more lethal than aspirin contained within.

"What could it be?" Mac said, shaking his head. Bobby began to move once more, sitting up with a dazed look on his face.

"Wow, that was intense," Bobby said, shivering. "Bobby! Are you alright?" Mac said, touchind Bobby's face with his right hand.

"Yeah, Dad, I'm just fine. I've never felt better," Bobby said.

"You scared the heck out of...my god, what happened to your eyes?" Mac said.

"What do you mean?" Bobby asked.

"Holy crap, your eyes are black, kid," Ramos said. "What did you do?" But he looked over at the unconscious form of his brother and figured it out. He shook his head. "Foolishness."

"Dad, you get to turn into a wolven with superhuman strength and speed, Ramos. You shoot purple fire from your hands, and even Lilith gets to shoot orange fire from hers, so can you blame me?" Bobby said. "You are tampering with forces you can't possibly comprehend, Bobby. Your father was fortunate not to have been killed when Gregor tapped into him," Ramos said.

Laughter rang out in the night around them, cruel and cold, breaking the silence. Mac stood, turning around in circles, his senses on full alert. They formed a circle around the children with their backs toward each other. Claws and teeth bared for the impending attack, and then, as suddenly as it had begun, the laughter stopped. Dark clouds parted overhead, and the moon shone, casting light on the beach and the shadowy figure standing twenty feet from where Bobby sat.

"I was wondering how I would pay you back for killing my brother, but your son did it for me," The figure said and stepped into the cold moonlight.

"Who are you? You're not Baal," Lilith asked.

She raised her bow.

"I've been burning for over a hundred years. There's no need to waste your arrow, Lilith." The man walked closer, and they could see large gray wings attached to his back that spread wide for a moment and then curled behind him.

He stood thirteen feet tall, with smoldering eyes, and around his waist was a battle skirt so long that when he moved, it seemed as if he were floating on air. "Look in my eyes, Colonel MacDonald, and tell me who you see," The apparition said.

"You have no sway over me, foul being!" Mac said, readying his claws for attack.

Serena held his rifle, aiming it at the strange man, but she lay down on the ground, staying still. When the newcomer entered the purple orb of Ramos's magical light, Mac knew in an instant that he was speaking with Major Tom Harper, and his mind traveled back to the last time they had spoken. It was when he rescued the children from the underground bunker in New Mexico. The scar from his right eye down to the chin was still there, and his facial features were all the same, but he was changed and morphed into some arcane creature from another realm.

"Harper," Mac said, his voice a whisper. "My God, what did they do to you?"

"Call me Azazel. And Do? They didn't *do* anything but set me free from a world of torment. I would have been dead if not for Lucifer. He found me with a pistol in my mouth, my finger on the trigger, and my bags packed for the afterlife. I'll admit, when you first meet the master, it's a daunting, frightening experience. But, when he shows you the power of Hell and extends an invitation to join him, you don't just refuse the offer. "They twisted your mind," Mac said.

"That was already twisted by the circumstances in which we were left. The transformation wasn't without pain, Colonel, but I feel like I made the right decision in the end. You left us all here to die when you closed that cosmic portal," Harper said.

"I thought you had crossed over with the rest of the elites. I was too distracted to worry about you and your inability to walk through a door, Major." Mac asked.

"I went back down the elevator to retrieve the scrapbook of memories your daughter left in the television room, and when I came back up, you were all gone."

"The portals were opened long after you should have been dead, Harper. I'm not buying this. It's a trick," Mac said.

"Daddy, I asked Major Harper to go back and get my book. I'm so sorry. I forgot about it, and you went back," Serena said. She was wrapped around her father's leg.

"See, I told you. Abandoning me was not easy to get over, but when Lucifer came to me, on the edge of my bed, with that gun in my mouth, and asked for my help, well, I said, sure! All I had to do was trade one form for another, wait for the gateways to open, and watch humanity burn," Azazel said. "I'm sorry I forgot about you," Serena said.

"It all worked out in the end, dear," Azazel said. He raised his powerful, muscular arms above his head. Mac readied for an attack. Behind Azazel, a portal opened to a world of fire and brimstone, where volcanoes spewed fire into a darkened sky.

Piles of bleached bones that had once been humans, reptilians, and hosts of others were heaped into refuse stacks that stretched for miles, like a junkyard for bodies.

Winged gargoyles, dragons, and walking abominations with teeth and claws so massive they would blot out the sun and moon trundled through the fiery landscape. Mac could hear them grunting and groaning inside his head— hungry, deadly, ferocious predators on a hunt for the living. Hordes of demons were marching in formation, an army of darkness born in the bowels of a world destroyed and forgotten by even the creator.

"Leave us alone or die," Ramos said.

"Yes, demon, you are outnumbered," Lilith said. "I agree, Harper; cut the monologue and get on with whatever it is you came here to do, or go away,"

Mac said.

"I'm not here to fight with any of you, just simply to welcome you back to the new Earth. Although I'd be more concerned with what's happening to your son right now if I were you, Colonel," Harper said.

Bobby had begun to transform before their eyes, and as he did, he looked up at the moon and howled. His eyes were black as deep space, and the skin on his body writhed and wriggled. The purple strands winding through his brain blackened, poisoning his mind. He doubled over in pain and screamed as a black spike erupted from his spine, and a long black tail grew behind him. It was tipped with a spade- shaped bone, and his legs began to extend as his formerly white skin blackened. Bobby's maw grew out, and his teeth became like razors, sharp and terrifying.

"Dad! Help," Bobby moaned.

"What did you do to my son, Harper?" Mac said. "I did nothing, as I said before. Your sleeping wolf friend ate part of a demon at Myrtle Beach and poisoned his blood. How he hasn't turned into a demon yet is beyond me, but this is *sooo* much better. The second your son injected himself with that tainted blood, he was mine, and soon he'll forgeg he ever was human," Harper said.

He laughed as Bobby completed his transformation and stood eleven feet tall, much taler than all but Azazel. Bobby had become a hybrid wolven demon, and as he looked down at his blackened skin, he howled again in a long, low, mournful tone before sprouting black, thick, coarse fur, covering him in a thick blanket. Bobby sported the ears of a wolf, and foot-long horns now jutted from his forehead.

"Are you ready to go home, Bobby?" Azazel asked.

"Dad, what's happening to me?" Bobby asked. "You leave my boy alone, Harper!" Mac said. "I told you to call me Azazel!" Azazel said.

Mac felt a pang of sorrow for his son and immediately turned it into feral rage. Mac leaped for Azazel and slammed into the much taller man with full force. Harper stood like a stone golem as Mac bounced off his rigid body and fell to the ground, and then, with a flick of his wrist, Azazel tossed Mac out into the ocean, far beyond the reef.

"You didn't think it would be that easy, did you? I've got more powerful friends than you, MacDonald. Lucifer gave me so much power! I'll be seeing you, commander," Harper said.

The voice came from inside his head as Mac swam wildly for shore. The thought of mega-sharks unseen in the deep black water eating him as a midnight snack caused an adrenaline surge, and his legs propelled him through the high waves back to shore. Ramos blasted Azazel with his purple fire as Lilith unleashed hers, knocking him backward.

"You've underestimated your enemy," Ramos said, hurling another fireball at Azazel.

This one sent him tumbling past his portal to Hell and into the ocean, where steam began to rise off his body. He stood in the tide, and from his hands, he fired a volley of black daggers at Ramos, who enveloped them with purple light and disintegrated the thrown weapons. Ramos was about to lob another fireball when Lilith fired a lightning arrow at Azazel, but her missile was knocked out of the air by a black blur as the creature that was Bobby defended Azazel.

Bobby rolled across the sand, turned on Lilith, and growled at her with onyx black eyes and white fangs. His muscles rippled like that of a bodybuilder flexing and tensed just before he leaped through the air once more. Ramos, in a moment of frustrated battle rage, let a massive burst of energy fly forth, catching Bobby in the rib cage. The ensuing blast knocked Bobby through the portal to Azazel's fiery world of horrors and onto his back. For a moment, Bobby returned to his former self, and Ramos could see the outline of the human face beneath the demonic wolven monster.

"Dad? Where am I? What have I done?" Bobby said, holding his hands outstretched. "You have five days to reach your son before he becomes a demon forever," Azazel said. "And next time, Colonel, I won't be alone."

Azazel pointed to the creatures inside his world, and as Mac ran for the portal to retrieve his son, Azazel dived through, and the gateway vanished.

"No!" Mac screamed. "I lost my son! We've got to get him!"

He was beside himself with anger and fear for his little boy. Mac could no longer control his language or his fists, and he pounded the sand until blood streaked his knuckles and tears streamed from his eyes as he wove a tapestry of curse words into the night.

"Mac! You have to get control of yourself. Your son is still alive, and we still have the Tablet of Destinies. We all need to complete this mission, which may be the only way to save your son," Lilith said.

"Bobby will be alright for the next five days, but we need to move out in the morning," Jasmine said. "If you all want to get some sleep, I'll stand watch tonight," Lilith said. She walked over and put her arm around Mac. He leaned into her embrace and sighed.

"She's right; we'll lose it if we don't get some shuteye. I'm just a little scared right now, is all, and I have no idea how I'm supposed to get any sleep with the image of my son in Hell," Mac said.

"You will sleep safe tonight; I'll be watching over all of you," Lilith said.

Ramos cast a spell of sleeping over everyone but Lilith, and they lay down for a night of dreamless, restful slumber under the stars. As Mac and Serena slept next to Ramos, Lilith sat on an outcropping of rocks, watched lightning strike the ocean miles away from shore, and thought for the first time in a hundred years about how much she missed her beautiful creator Ninhursag.

CHAPTER 9

MAC AWOKE WITH A START and found himself before a grey, twenty-foot-tall stone door with two handles carved into the rock. He stood alone before this megalithic oddity and found thick, dark woods surrounding him. The door stood as the gateway into another world, and when he turned around to go, Mac realized he was before the same bleak portal he had seen in his previous dream. Tall trees, black, twisted, and rotten, stood against him on the other side of the gate. He listened quietly, and he could hear someone calling his name.

Mac wanted to follow the voice, toss open the gate and run through, abandon his quest, and retire to the shadow world. A voice whispered in his ear to walk toward the entrance, but he knew with instinctual surety that the land awaiting him on the other side was for those who could not wait for the sweet embrace of death to take them.

This was the world of suicides and misery, and as a lonely mist swept the ground on the other side of the black, wrought iron gate, Mac turned his back on it. That existence had no future, but something about the door still intrigued him. There was a task at hand, but he could not remember it. He placed his palm against the door and felt warmth as if the stone were heated from the other side. A high and robust wall stretched east and west toward the horizon into infinity. And there he was, stuck between a stone door and an iron gate.

"Mac," A voice whispered.

It was low and ominous and sent a chill up Mac's spine. He turned to see that the iron gate was open, and the figure of a woman stood facing him. She wore a black funeral dress, and a veil covered her face, obscuring her features.

"Hello? Who's there?" Mac said. A cold wind greeted his request, but the figure did not reply. Mac thought about A Christmas Carol and the ghost of Christmas past.

Her right hand lifted, and she pointed toward the door behind him, head still bowed. Mac turned back to the stone door and put his right hand on the right door handle.

"This has to weigh twenty tons. How am I supposed to open it?" Mac said, turning back to the specter, but no one was there. He pulled, and he could hear screaming from the other side as the door slid open easily.

He turned back once more and saw what looked like green leaves sprouting from the blackened husks of what were once trees beyond the gate. Mac sighed and turned toward the entrance. As he walked inside, the door closed behind him with whisper-like silence.

He was now trapped inside a grand hallway that led down into blackness, and no matter how he pushed the door he had come in through, it would not budge. Mac walked the path down the hallway, and as he did, the screaming became more pronounced and louder, and he could hear those suffering pleading to be set free. Thick and punishing sulfur stung his nostrils, and Mac wondered if he was indeed walking into Hell. The walls were illuminated by flickering orange-red light at the passage's end, so he continued forward. Curiosity and a sense of fate drove him onward as his heartbeat thumped out a rhythmic staccato, echoing the fear inside him.

"Bobby's here," Mac said.

Light grew at the end of the corridor, and there was a bend to the left as he neared the end. Turning the corner, Mac was greeted by the vision of another world within a world, but unlike Valuria, the fiery world below resembled tales from ancient times. This place was the last stop for the poor unfortunates condemned to burn. Mac stood atop a cliff, staring down into a lake of molten rock where tortured screams from millions of trapped souls rose toward the ceiling of the enormous cavern. To his right, a path led to a shoreline far below, where molten lava washed up on the land like ocean waves. The ferryman stood aboard his ancient boat, waiting for the next fare. Mac felt like he was walking into Dante's Inferno. The damned, consumed by fire, clambered over each other in their futile attempts to swim ashore, their skin melting off like hot wax over flesh and bone. Each time a poor soul floated two feet forward, they vanished and reappeared back to where they began.

Mac walked down to the ferryman's boat and stood before him. Standing fifteen feet tall, garbed in a hooded cloak with skeletal hands extending beyond the sleeves, the sailor regarded Mac from behind the darkness of his ragged, aged hood. With an outstretched hand, he stood waiting in silence for payment.

"Pay the toooooooll," The ferryman said. "I've got no money," Mac said.

"Pay the toooooooll and crossssss the laaaaaake," The ferryman said. His voice was hoarse and drawn out.

"Daaad!" Bobby's voice came from the other side of the lake.

"Bobby!" Mac said. His eyes darted to a tunnel on the other side of the fire lake and back to the ferryman. "The coin, pleeease," The ferryman said.

"Not a chance, pal," Mac said. He leaped forward onto the raft and knocked the cloaked skeletal figure into the pyroclastic lake. "Take a swim," he said.

The ferryman let out a wretched squeal as he burst into flames, and the grabbing, greedy hands of the damned reached up with supernatural fervor to pull him under their roiling, molten rock lake. Mac stepped forward, preparing to leap toward the raft as he heard his name on the hot wind, calling from somewhere far away. He turned toward the dark tunnel on the other side, where Bobby most assuredly awaited rescue, and he felt his instincts telling him to get on the raft.

"Maaaac! Where are you?" Lilith said.

It sounded like her voice was coming through a tube, and he felt himself drawn backward. Mac opened his eyes and was lying on the sandy beach, staring up at a night sky blanketed with millions of tiny points of light. Lilith ran over to him and began patting his chest and arms.

"Wha...?" Mac said.

"You're smoking! My god, where did you go?" Lilith asked. She looked shocked, and he began to wonder if what he had experienced was, in fact, a dream or if he had been standing at the doorway to the underworld. She stopped patting him down and looked into his eyes. "You vanished right before my eyes, Mac."

"I was at the doorway to the underworld, Hell, or whatever you want to call it. Bobby called my name from beyond the lake of fire, so I tried to get him, but then I heard your voice. I remember being pulled backward by the sound, but nothing more," Mac said.

"It's good you listened to my voice and came back. You're no match for the being that lives in that realm, not alone anyway," Lilith said.

"It seemed like a dream," Mac said.

"You smell like a cooked cat, and after I called for you, your body faded from where you were. This was no dream, and I've never seen anything like it," Lilith said.

"Maybe we'll get some answers from the faeries," Mac said. Lilith held him close to her.

"You're the only man I've ever loved. Over the millennia, I've almost lost the ability to feel emotion, and I know I can seem cold and indifferent, but I would scour the planet for you. When you vanished, I thought I'd lost you, Mac," Lilith said.

She pulled away from him, and a glint of light reflected off a single tear as it traced down her left cheek. He could feel her need, and their souls connected like the roots of two trees growing into one another.

"After Carol died, I thought I'd never love again. The pain was too deep, and we'd been together for so long, and I do know what you mean about losing the ability to feel," Mac said.

"And how do you feel about me?" Lilith asked. "I believe I'm deeply in love with you as well, Lilith," Mac said. She hugged him.

"This is touching you guys; I think I'm going to cry," Dante said. He propped himself up on his left elbow, watching them and shaking his head. "My head is ringing like a bell,"

"Welcome back, funny man," Mac said and laughed. Mac and Lilith explained what Dante had missed the previous night while he lay unconscious on the sand.

"I'm so sorry, Mac. My blood turned your son into a demon?" Dante asked.

"It's not your fault, my friend. Bobby was meddling where he should not have been, but the fact remains that I've got to get him before he turns forever. I only have five days," Mac said.

The sun rose, and the party began to awaken to the fresh salt air of a new day. Fall was approaching, and the breeze blowing off the sea carried a refreshing chill. Mac could see the ruins of abandoned oil rigs and rusted buildings on stilts resembling oceanic forts. The stilt buildings were round and were fifty meters in diameter, a testament to the engineering prowess of Mac's contemporaries. Something big and black swam in between the rig and fort supports. A dorsal fin rose above the water line, but the rest of the aquatic behemoth played in the shadows of early morning shade.

"Anyone for a swim?" Dante asked. His joke fell flat, and although Ramos smiled, he shook his head. "Fine, I'm going to go look for food. I'm starving," Dante said as he walked off into the forest behind their camp.

Jasmine walked over to Mac and Lilith, sitting beside Serena, consoling her.

"Sweetie, your brother is going to be fine. We've got plenty of time, and this will all be over soon," Mac said.

"Dad, I miss our old life. I want to return to the farm and forget this happened," Serena said.

"Yeah, I know what you mean. Look, even if we could go back there right now, to that time, we wouldn't be the same people, and I have a feeling this adventure will stay with all of us for the rest of our lives," Mac said.

"I want to see Mom," Serena said. "I do, too. But she's gone, Serena," Mac said. "She comes to me when I dream. I can see her through a golden gate, and she's in a green dress," Serena said.

"You do? Have you ever talked to her?" Mac asked. He thought of the black wrought iron bars he had stared through in his dreams to that bleak, dead world.

"Sometimes, she tells me to make sure I take care of you," Serena said.

"That sounds like her. Does she say anything else?" Mac asked.

"Mom tells me lots of things, Daddy. She told me you and Bobby were in trouble, but it'll be OK," Serena said. She stared despondently down at the ground, and Mac felt a white streak crawl up his spine. He saw the specter in black in his mind again, but he said nothing to her about it.

"She mentioned Bobby?" Mac asked.

"Yeah, he sees her, too," Serena said. Mac felt his longing for Carol grow in intensity. Nothing made sense anymore.

"Your mom was right that it will be OK, regardless of the outcome. Pretty soon, we'll find out how this little adventure ends," Mac said. He smiled and hugged his daughter. "Dad, I don't want you or Bobby to die," Serena said.

"Well, I think it's like my dad used to tell me. We all move on eventually because nothing lives forever except for the Earth and the clouds. What matters is what you do with your time while you're here. The folks that remember you fondly are what make a life well lived. Does that make sense?" Mac said.

"Yeah, but Daddy, are we going to get Bobby back? That man who took him seemed...angry like he might hurt him," Serena said. Mac thought about his late wife's prophetic words, and an involuntary shiver ran through him.

"Let's just focus on getting him back and try not to overthink it, OK? It'll be what it's going to be," Mac said. He felt a flood of sadness overcome him for only a moment, and then Dante walked back through the trees with two giant snapping turtles under his arms.

"I found these things wandering around by a pool of dark water back there. Whatever they are, they look delicious, and they even come with their cooking shells, Dante said. He threw them into the center of the camp.

"Those, my friend, are two of the biggest turtles I've ever seen. They'll make fine eating," Jasmine said. "She's right; those things are tasty. I'll find some wood, and we can build a fire," Mac said.

"We need to get moving soon. The entrance to the faerie world is around this island, but they keep moving the door so that it may take a while, and I don't want to be stuck in those woods at night," Jasmine said.

"You should see some of the fun things that come out at night on Eritria. Kid-sized spiders, for instance," Mac said.

"The faeries come out at night around here, and if they find you sleeping, they steal your soul," Jasmine said.

"Right, I'll take the spiders," Mac said. "Alright everyone, you heard the lady; we've got until nightfall,"

"What if we find them first?" Ramos asked. "We'll ask for a meeting with the queen. They'll have to grant it and let her decide our fate," Jasmine said.

"How will we know her if she looks like a goblin?" Mac asked.

"Queen Lalibala is no goblin," Lilith said. "You know her?" Jasmine asked.

"She's my cousin. Boys, keep your business to yourself when in her presence, or you'll end up dancing in a faerie circle, and we'll never see you again," Lilith said.

"That's uplifting and encouraging, but I think we can handle ourselves," Mac said. Dante and Ramos nodded and clapped Mac on the back.

"Trust me when I say she's very convincing," Lilith said.

Mac found firewood, and the two built a respectable campfire to cook Dante's turtles. When all were full, and the conversation lulled, Jasmine doused the fire and led them into the woods. The warm, bright morning sun danced on the branches and leaves, casting shadows that moved like people as a gentle breeze blew in from the shore. The forest air smelled of salt water and rotting leaves as they crunched and plodded through the dense brush.

"How are we supposed to find anything in here?

Too many plants!" Dante said.

"Shhh! Listen," Jasmine said. She held up a finger and cocked her head. "Do you hear the music?"

"I hear it," Lilith said. "Here we go."

They walked about a hundred more steps and reached a clearing in the woods. What they saw defied Mac's imagination and brought life to the words they had heard. Inside the clearing was a circle of small stones, and within the ring was a dancing, gibbering old man. Without a care in the world, he was twirling and flapping his arms to an invisible orchestra. Out of his mind, insane, he did not notice the party as they approached.

"Don't enter the circle, or your mind will be transported to that man's world. You'll end up like this guy," Jasmine said. "And it looks like he's been here for a while."

The man had danced around the faerie circle so many times that his feet had created a twelve-inch rut in the dirt.

"How long do you think he's been here?" Serena asked.

"I don't know. How long would it take you to dig a foot-deep hole with your feet by walking around and around in a circle?" Jasmine answered.

"Years," Ramos whispered.

"Can't someone knock him out of it? One of us throws the other, or we tie a log up in a tree and sail it at him like a battering ram?" Dante asked.

"The magic's too strong inside the circle. It's an energy field, and anything that goes in will be just as trapped as he is," Jasmine said.

"So, this guy just dances around for eternity?" Mac asked.

"Until they finish draining his energy, yeah. He was dead the moment he entered," Jasmine said. "This type of thing is exactly why we went to war with the faeries," Dante said.

"Dante, Shhh," Ramos said.

"I will not shut up; these people are the catalyst for our Marduk's downfall and the reason we were split into five tribes!"

"What?" Lilith asked.

"That's ancient history, and we are not on Eritria anymore. ," Ramos said.

"You're right, but is this evidence that these people are any better?" Dante said.

A hatch opened beside a tall oak tree on the other side of the circle, and a small man, about three feet tall, popped his head out of the underground entryway. He had not noticed the party yet and walked around the circle, adjusting the stones. His skin was light green, and he had spindly arms and legs with hunched shoulders, giving him the appearance of an old man, but his movement was agile and quick, like that of a sprite. The little man's facial features were almost human.

"Stay here for a minute," Lilith said. Lilith approached the tiny man, and as she snapped a stick with her foot, his head rose with a start. He turned to run for his hole.

"Stay away!" The man yelled. "Please don't go. I wish to have a word with your queen," Lilith said. The man was back at his hatch, preparing to leap down the hole. "Tell her Lilith seeks her counsel,"

The faerie looked back at her again, scowled, and screamed at her as he jumped down the hole. The old man in the circle continued to dance to the rhythmic faerie drums and a flute that became louder the closer Lilith walked toward him.

"You made an impression on that little guy," Jasmine said.

"We may not have time for niceties. Let's follow him down the hole," Mac said.

" Give it a few minutes, Lilith said.

Ramos's head began to hurt again, and he covered his face with the hood of his robe to hide the pain.

"You alright?" Dante asked. "Fine," Ramos said.

"That's a lie, what's wrong?" Dante asked. "There's a psychic imbalance on this planet thae does not want us here. I feel it in the air and around each turn. I feel it is knocking on the door of my mind," Ramos spoke.

"I know. I sense it, too," Dante said.

"We don't belong here, Dante. If we don't leave soon, I fear for our lives," Ramos said. Ramos' eyes seethed purple flame as if to validate his words until he closed them tight. "My magic is becoming uncontrollable, Dante,"

"We'll get out of here, Ramos. As soon as we help Mac save his world, we will find a way back to Eritria. There has to be a way home," Dante said.

Jasmine walked around the circle, careful not to step inside, and stopped at the place where the hatch had once been. Nothing remained but a patch of grass.

"They don't leave trails to follow; that's why nobody believes the faeries exist until they see one," Lilith said.

"Yeah, thanks, I already knew that," Jasmine said.

"No offense; it's been a long year," Lilith said.

A breeze blew through the trees, and suddenly, they could hear music surrounding them as the forest floor moved. Hundreds of faerie holes opened, and out of each sprung a faerie wielding a small wooden wand. They looked like long wooden matchsticks to Mac until one of the faeries fired a small green bolt out of one with the flick of his wrist. It struck a tree beside Dante, and he bared his claws, growling at the little man, preparing to attack.

"Dante, stand down," Mac said. "Stop in the name of the queen!" One faerie man said.

"What's the meaning of this? We came here in peace," Jasmine said.

"Trespassers!" Another faerie man said.

The adventurers prepared to defend their lives as a golden light appeared from beyond the circle, grew brighter, and began to move like a wisp on the wind. The entity approaching was so brilliant it seemed to the party as if a star had fallen from heaven and found a home on Earth. The music of the woods became a peaceful, lulling, rhythmic vibration.

"Pretty music," Dante said.

"Yes, it's so tranquil. Peaceful and..." Mac said. He yawned and stood grinning as the ball of light floated to within three feet of them. The ball of light vanished with an audible pop, revealing the passenger within.

The woman before them was gorgeous, fair- skinned, and five feet tall, with long blond hair. She dwarfed the little men gathered around her feet.

She wore a green satin gown with runes stitched into it that shone like holographic images as she moved. Her long hair draped down the back of her dress in loose curls, and as Mac looked into her deep blue eyes, the strange woman's hypnotic gaze entranced him. Lilith stood beside him and jammed his leg with the end of her bow, giving the Colonel a massive, trance-breaking Charlie horse.

"Ouch! What the..." Mac said.

"Do you want to end up like that guy over there, or worse?" Lilith said. She stepped toward the serenely smiling woman.

"Queen Lalibala, it's been a long time," Lilith said and began to bow.

"Oh, stop it, Lilith. You're family; you don't need to bow to me," Lalibala said.

She drifted to the ground and approached the winged, brunette beauty, embracing her with both arms. Lilith returned the gesture.

"It's been so long, cousin. Please, come inside," Lalibala snapped her fingers, and in an instant, the entire party stood in a great hall in Lalibala's underground castle.

"What do you think?" Lalibala said.

High stone walls and pillars carved from basalt reached up hundreds of feet into darkness and held up the ceiling of Earth above their heads. Each stone had been meticulously cut and stood above the other with such close tolerance that Mac doubted he could get a strand of hair between them. Runes etched into the stones reminded Mac of the megalithic structures from lost civilizations, each telling a story within the carving. The great hall, more expansive than a six-lane freeway, turned to the left and right, leading into the Faerie city.

Mac turned to face Lalibala and was stunned by the forty-foot stone statue of *her* standing behind a throne carved from mahogany and gilded with jewels.

"Lilith, it's been over twelve thousand years since I've seen you. How have you been?" Lalibala asked. She led the party to a long table and chairs as she spoke.

"I've been living on another planet, in exile," Lilith said.

"So, how did you meet these people?" The queen asked, turning to Mac.

"I met them on Eritria and assisted the wolven in a war for their world."

"I want to know more about what happened to the humans, Mac. We were sleeping during that age and woke up one day to the nightmare above ground," Lalibala said.

"What would you like to know? I'll tell you what I remember," Mac said.

"What happened? What caused this catastrophe?" Lalibala asked.

"We failed," Mac said. "We threw our future away because of greed and obsession for physical possessions. First came the freak lightning storms, then tornadoes, and next the worldwide tsunamis and war among our people," Mac said.

"What did you do?" Lalibala asked.

"I wish I could tell you we got together and started to work on the problem as a world community. But what we did was begin to kill each other in the streets and panic like animals. War inevitably erupted over resources like fuel and water, and at first, it was contained to the big cities, but like dominoes falling in a row, the trouble moved out into smaller towns and burgs. The freak storms had everyone thinking that the biblical end times were coming, so they created a self-fulfilling prophecy of death and destruction,"

"Things fell apart because of resource wars?" Lalibala asked.

"Not just that, humanity polluted the environment with fertilizers, other chemicals, and plastic trash to the extent that our environment could no longer sustain us. We had a population of thirteen billion people, and all of us were competing for the same land, food, and water. As a last resort to save a handful of citizens, the people who hired me decided to use a device they found aboard an ET spacecraft, and it allowed us to open a portal back to Earth from Eritria, which was a planet we found to be acceptable for human life." "You saved the remaining humans?" Lalibala asked.

"Not exactly; the wealthy people who commissioned the work never intended to bring the rest of humanity over. The ultra-wealthy hired an army of contract killers to protect them, and then once they were across the threshold with their tanks, bombs, and guns, the gate was closed and then stolen. By the time we got it back and opened it again, one hundred and fifty years had passed over here," Mac said.

"That's an entertaining story, and it does answer some questions, but it doesn't quite explain why you're on my island,"

"We need your help, Lalibala," Lilith asked. "Why should I help you?" Lalibala asked. Mat motioned for Serena to come over, and then removed the Tablet of Destiny from her backpack and held it up for the queen to see. Her mouth dropped in surprise.

"Because we're here to save the planet," Mac said.

CHAPTER 10

"SO, YOU'VE FOUND ONE OF the six tablets?" Lalibala asked.

"It's the last of them; the only other remaining tablet is safe inside a tower underground on Eritria," Lilith said.

"And the other four?" Lalibala asked. "Broken in a war long ago," Lilith said.

"I see. While that's impressive, what do you intend to do with it? All of my people tell me we're dealing with inter-dimensional beings and Lucifer himself," Lalibala said. Mac cleared his throat and got the queen's attention. "Back in Valuria, I had a dream, a vision, whatever you want to call it, that I was aboard a wooden ship, and we had the tablet in our possession. The Great Pyramid of Giza was on the horizon, and I knew it would be ready when we arrived. Next, I saw that a great network of pyramids would begin to operate or communicate once more.," Mac said. Lalibala nodded.

"What do you need from me if you already have one of the sacred tablets?" Lalibala asked.

"We were hoping that you could help us get to the land called Egypt so that we can finish what we came here to do, cousin," Lilith said.

Lalibala seemed to think about it for a moment, reflecting on the question. "There is a way, but it's dangerous, and I can't guarantee your safety," Lalibala said.

"What is it?" Dante asked.

"You'll have to go through the Portal of Xannar," Lalibala said.

"OK, what's that?" Mac asked. He felt an irresistible raw, animal lust for the queen and heard Lilith's warning in his mind.

"Xannar is a portal keeper who lives deep inside the Earth, very close to the core of this planet. He has extraordinary power, and if you can convince him not to kill you, he may help," "I've heard of him, but he doesn't work well with others. Are you sure this is the only way?" Lilith asked. "You've been on this planet since before the dawn of man, and our hope lies with Xannar? From all I've heard, he is not to be trusted."

"Who is Xannar?" Serena asked.

"He was a friend to the faerie people millions of years ago, so far back that the moon had not yet been set into orbit around the Earth. Xannar showed us how to tap into the magical power of this planet and use the energy to create trees, plants, and animals. He's a shepherd of nature and a creator, but grouchy and temperamental," Lalibala said.

"Is Xannar a bad man?" Serena asked.

Lalibala shook her head. "Xannar is not a man, but a celestial being who crosses between our dimension and many others. He became very frustrated with this realm at the end of the first age of man and vanished from it. He may be able to help, but you'll have to find him, and I'll warn you, he laid traps long ago for those who ever tried to seek him out."

"Traps? Why is everything so difficult? Can't you summon him or something?" Dante asked.

Mac began to feel an irresistible urge to reach out to Lalibala and kiss her. He longed to stroke her soft skin, get closer, smell the sweet fragrance of her hair, and that's when Lilith kicked him in the ankle. Mac turned to her, annoyed, in wolven form once more, and stopped cold when he saw the look of warning in her eyes. He thought about the man dancing above them and his deep, rutted circle. "I cannot. Xannar will not respond to telekinetic communication. He feels it's an invasion of his privacy. You'll have to go and seek him out. If he chooses to help, he'll open a portal and send you on your way,"

"That's what we'll do then. Thank you, Lalibala. Can you please point the way?" Lilith said. You have such fine skin, my lady," Ramos said. His eyes were wide, staring, focused only on Lalibala. He stepped toward her.

"Would you like to touch it, warlock?" Lalibala said.

"I ask for a night alone with you, queen," Ramos said.

"Your friends are welcome to run along, and your wish is granted. Come closer and kiss me," Lalibala said.

"So sweet, the music, I can hear music," Ramos said. "It's calming."

Lalibala began to sing in a sweet, soft tone. It was a lullaby, although no one else in the party could hear her words or the flute that had begun to play for Ramos. He was entranced and crept forward. Dante stood staring at his brother, confused.

"What's wrong with him?" Dante asked. Mac knew because he had also begun to hear her flutes just before Lilith kicked him in the ankle.

"I hope you're not going to hold this against me, my friend," Mac said, hitting Ramos in the side of his jaw with a wide left-handed haymaker. The wolven warlock toppled over onto his side and looked up momentarily, confusion written across his face.

"What just happened?" Ramos asked. "Mac saved your life," Lilith said.

"The queen was seducing you; sorry, I had to hit ya," Mac said.

"Well, I can't win them all," Lalibala said and giggled.

"Lady, are you the devil?" Ramos asked. "Lucifer does not seduce. He twists and burnc with fire, but you'd love being my slave, I promise you that. Not one more care in the world for the rest of your days," Lalibala said.

"You boys are a mess. See what I have to deal with?" Lilith said. Lalibala smiled.

"Walk through the tunnel behind me until you come to a spring in the rocks, and then follow the bend right for about a mile. You'll run into the staircase leading down, but after that, you'll have to deal with the traps Xannar left behind when he abandoned our world," Lalibala said.

"How long ago did you say he left?" Ramos asked.

"Xannar has not been seen for about three million years, maybe longer," Lalibala said and walked over to a box on the shelf behind her ornate throne. After a moment, she produced a small metal band. "Here, take this ring. It's the sigil of Lalibala and will guide you toward Xannar. If it turns green, you are getting close," Lalibala said, handing the ring to Lilith.

"Why does she get to wear it?" Dante asked. "Because Lilith is one of the first immortals created by our ancestors, the sky gods, and if you tried to put it on the vibratory energy would kill you in a matter of minutes,"

"Got it. Everyone except Lilith, stay away from that ring," Dante said.

The wall began to groan, and quake, the rock separated into a split that ran from ceiling to floor, and as it did, the odor of sulfur stung their nostrils. "We're not walking into a chamber of poisonous vapor, are we?" Ramos asked.

"No, my friends, there's a volcanic vein down there, but the path bridges it, and you'll be fine in the tunnel as long as you stay close to the walls," Lalibala said.

Mac walked forward, fascinated by the queen's power.

"The people of my time would not believe this if they saw it with their own eyes," Mac said.

"When you pass beyond the opening, the wall will reseal, and you'll be on your own for the rest of your journey. May your quest bring balance back to our world," Lalibala said.

Lilith, the last in line, turned and embraced her cousin. "Thank you, Lalibala. I love you, and we will meet again soon," Lilith said.

Lilith bade farewell to her cousin, the fairy queen, who followed behind Jasmine halfway through the opening and shrouded in darkness. Dante had already removed the light gem from his pouch and held it above his head to give the party light. Lilith joined Jasmine and the rest of the group, and then the cracked wall sealed behind them with a slow creak, like old furniture moving across a wooden floor.

"And they were never seen again," Mac said, his voice echoing off the cold rock walls. He watched the queen vanish; several meters of stone closed her silhouette. He turned toward Lilith.

"What?" Lilith asked. "I used to watch these ridiculous horror movies when I was a kid, and in some of them, the main character would say that line," Mac said. He was shaking his head and grinning.

"I don't get it," Lilith said.

"I'll explain it someday. Let's get going; we only have four days left to save Bobby," Mac said.

Dante led the way through a long, deep passage into the darkness, where madness awaited them on their way to Xannar. The passage quickly evolved from a tunnel to an elaborate system of hallways carved from stone, held up with magnificent rock pillars. Faces of trolls, elves, faeries, centaurs, mole men, wolven, humans, and satyrs were carved expertly into the stone as if by diamond blade or laser. The rock floor ended, and a cobblestone walkway began, winding around the pillars as they rose toward the black ceiling.

"I see all manner of races represented down here.

What is this place?" Ramos asked.

A gigantic granite archway greeted them at the end of a winding tunnel. In the center of the arch was the massive stone head ram head, with curling horns that swept down beside its head, and in the middle of its forehead were two three-foot-long spiked horns. The stone head of this beast fixed them with a baleful gaze. "What is that?!" Dante asked.

"My guess is Xannar," Jasmine said. "He looks angry," Serena said.

"Those eyes are watching us," Dante said.

"I know, they have been since we stepped into this chamber," Ramos said.

"Guys, are you coming?" Lilith asked. The giant stone head moved.

"We've got a problem," Dante said and pointed up.

The stone archway shuddered and groaned while the mouth opened and closed as pebbles fell and bounced across the floor.

"The archway is collapsing! Everyone get out of the way!" Jasmine yelled.

The spirit within the rock lurched forward in a psychedelic array of colors as the party stood frozen in fear. First, an arm formed, then a torso, and then legs and feet. A supernatural horror loomed over them like a giant golem, and there was nowhere to run if it decided to attack.

"What do you want?!" The massive stone creature asked.

Mac decided that someone had better speak fast. "We're here from the overworld, and we require assistance to save it from ruin! Are you Xannar?" Mac asked. "I am Xannar, and ruin is a strong word, human. It depends on your outlook because, from my point of view, they did me a favor by wiping out your kind. Now, GO AWAY, or I'll hurl you into oblivion," Xannar said. His voice was a roaring boom in the darkness. He turned to walk away. Serena stepped in front of her father and spoke next.

"Please, sir, you have to help us. My brother is going to be turned into a demon in less than four days, and we really can repair the damage to Earth," Serena said.

"I've seen stars born, live, and die in my long life. If you can impress me, I'll help you restore the planet," Xannar said. Serena pulled out the Tablet of Destinies and showed it to him.

"We have to get to the Great Pyramid; it's in Egypt," Serena said. Xannar's frown turned into a blank stare as he marveled at the object.

"You've got one of the six tablets. Impressive, since that was sent to a planet far from here a long, long time ago in human years," Xannar said. "Come here, girl,"

"Please, don't hurt my daughter," Mac said. His heart raced with adrenaline as Xannar reached out his massive stone hand.

"I'm not going to hurt any of you," Xannar said, taking Serena by her hand. "I'm going to show you who you are, and you'll do that for yourselves." Serena took his hand, and a moment later, her eyes began to glow with white light. Xannar turned her toward the rest of the group, and the light burst from Serena's eyes, which entered theirs as they all stood frozen in place.

"If you survive, I'll give you passage to Egypt." Mac tumbled through the blackness of space and time in a starless void that held him weightless, naked, and alone.

Hundreds of years passed in silence as his mind went blank. No more nightmares or bad memories; he was in the womb once more. A calm, tranquil feeling floated over him as Mac's mind became a radio for the universe, a beacon of information sending out waves of data. It was as it had always been in the beginning: darkness and solitude in the vastness of the universal vacuum.

Curled in the fetal position, eyes closed and fearless for the first time, Mac was cradled by the infinite multiverse. And then there was light. Mac opened his eyes and saw the ground forming. It was pixilated at first, like a video game trying to reform after a glitch, and then everything became clear.

Mac floated to the ground and found that he was wandering in the desert of New Mexico in his black flight suit. The wind picked up as he walked, blowing sand around his face. The sun overhead scorched the Earth upon which he strode, and he could see a building ahead of him. No, it was his hangar. He was back at *the cave*, and suddenly, his heartbeat faster like a tornado of fear. The hangar grew larger until he stood at one of the steel security doors, locked to intruders, the press, and conspiracy hunters, but today it was open. He felt for his security badge, which was always dangling from the lanyard around his neck.

He looked down to see the little zebra-striped pattern that signified his secret security level. Mac had access to alien ships, bodies, and other oddities that would have sent the public screaming or lashing out in religious hysteria as their idea of the creation myth crumbled in front of their eyes. The heavy door swung outward without any need to swipe his access card or look into the retinal scanner.

As he walked into the lit hangar, Mac could feel the desert heat baking his feet from inside his combat boots. Customarily staffed twenty-four hours a day, it was empty and alone.

"Hello?" Mac asked. His voice sounded tinny, foreign to his ears.

An empty tin can rolled across the floor, stopping at Mac's right foot. He looked down and saw it was an old soda can. He stepped around it and walked inside.

"Is anyone in here?" Mac asked. He heard the faint sound of someone screaming from far away. The door to the hanger closed behind him and latched. When he turned to open the door, it would not budge, and the hangar lights above his head went out one at a time until only two shone on another door locked with a biometric retinal scan and card reader. Mac followed the path and heard the screaming grow louder. The sound came from deep inside the cave; Mac knew the room number.

The biometric reader turned green as he approached, and the door slid back, revealing a set of elevator doors. Mac felt eyes on his back and turned to see if anyone was watching. A slip of black robe pulled back into darkness as the lights clicked off one by one. Mac caught the flash of a horned skull before everything went dark.

"Who's there?! What is this?" Mac said.

He felt tendrils of fear climbing up his spine as he turned from the specter of death and walked toward the opening elevator. Inside was a single dangling light bulb on a cord. It swung side to side in pendulum fashion, tossing shadows around as the moaning and screaming grew louder. Mac was terrified, and he knew what he would find if he descended in the metal box to his laboratory underground.

"It's OK; you got this," Mac said to himself. He stepped inside and pressed the only button on the right wall: a round arrow pointing down. Mac looked out into the blackness of the hanger and saw a wraith moving toward him with frightening speed. He pressed the button again, and the door closed too slowly, and his terror gripped him. Mac could see the skull of his tormentor, partially obscured by a black hood, with twin horns jutting from its forehead. It sliced through the air while Mac pressed the button faster, but the doors moved as if they were stuck in peanut butter.

"You belong to uuuuuuuussssss now!" The cloaked figure said and reached for the doors.

"You're not real!" Mac said.

The door shut as the robed skeletal figure reached through, but as the doors closed, it vanished. Mac stood against the back wall involuntarily— shrinking in fear— and looked down at his left arm, where three long, bloody scratches marked the skin. The screams faded as he felt the momentum of the elevator shift downward. Mac was in total silence.

"I think I liked the screaming better; at least I didn't feel it," Alone, he thought.

The doors opened, and he stepped out into a dark hallway with a few poorly maintained fluorescent lights and saw Carol. She was dressed in a white gown and wore a death shroud. "Carol?" Mac asked.

The ghostly figure turned and walked around the corner down a long hallway. Mac recognized the central processing center, the cell area, where potential candidates for the trials were drugged before confinement and ultimate demise in the chair. Mac followed the figure while the fluorescent lights above his head buzzed and flickered. The figure turned back to face him, and for a second, the shroud disappeared, and he could see the rotting face of his dead wife. Her eyes were gone, and greedy maggots crawled inside the deep, hollow sockets, each jockeying for a piece of flesh to consume. The cheeks were falling off, but enough of her face was left for a smile to form.

The corpse bride began to slide back down the hallway and around another corner. He walked ahead, moving past the cells where his consciousness experiments had been held captive, and as he did, hands reached out from behind the bars on every door. The reaching, rotting arms of those he condemned waved in the air, snatching for a piece of him.

Mac's vision flashed forward like a skip in a DVD, and he was sitting inside his chair. Unseen hands strapped his arms down, and when he looked left, there was a monitor attached to a crash cart with sharp instruments and syringes lying neatly in a row. The hangar door to the disposal room was open, and he could see thousands of barrels stacked on top of each other, but there was blood-red goo seeping out of them, pooling on the floor and slowly moving his way. When Mac turned his head back, he was face to face with a doctor wearing a surgical mask and a bloodstained, dirt-streaked white lab coat. He caught Mac looking at the coat.

"We're a production shop here, pal. Not much time for cleanup between contestants," The man said, his voice muffled.

"What do you mean? What contestants?" Mac asked.

"You're in luck, my friend, because we think you might be *the one* who can get us where we need to go. Now, relax and clear your mind. You're going to feel a quick pinch, and then you'll be good to go," The man said.

"What are you doing? This isn't right! Let me out of the chair!" Mac said.

He screamed at the placid-faced doctor as the reddish sludge on the floor formed many objects. They rose out of the mess and morphed into humans. The doctor caught him watching and saw the look of terror.

"These are just a few of the subjects you used in the past to further the plans of madmen. One...little...pinch," The doctor drove a needle into Mac's arm and turned a lever that was connected to a tube that ran down and up to a hanging bag of drugs. "There, now we're all set. Enjoy the ride, Colonel MacDonald,"

"What, wait, no...please, don't do this!" Mac said. A cast of thousands was now standing around, watching the show.

"I'll just turn this on, and you can see what's going on until you drop off to sleep," The doctor said. He moved his hand over to the monitor and turned it on. Half of the screen displayed a biorhythm monitor, and the other half was black.

"But we succeeded! The project was a success, and we found another planet. It didn't turn out like we thought, but you don't need to do this," Mac said. "Oh, I know, but that doesn't matter anymore.

The fertilizer barrels have to be filled," the doctor said, and his mask was removed.

Mac was staring back at his face, and just before he could scream, mind-rending pain shot through his temple as a stream of black fluid replaced the clear liquid in his IV. "Oops, forgot to give you the really good painkillers on the way in,"

"Oh my God! What did we do?" Mac said.

Space flew by on the monitor as Mac felt his consciousness pulled like taffy into the void. In moments, all reality surrounding his body faded to black, and he was soaring by planets, through black holes, passing clusters of stars giving birth to solar systems, and traveling through the circulatory system of the creator.

In the last moments of his life, he found the planet Eritria and glided down through her atmosphere. He viewed Wasatch Village and his former crewmates Kim and Stephanie, who were having a good relationship with the wolven. He saw a military installation north of the woods that could only have been built by humans and watched dark smoke churning from a chimney. The fires of human industry were alive on Eritria, and that was when Mac understood what he had done, and he knew who he was and what his part had been for the first time in his life.

Massive steel walls had been erected around the human village, and Mac could see traders from every race coming and going from the front gate. They were exchanging goods for small round gold coins the humans made from mining operations far up in the mountains. Mac knew that he was the destroyer of worlds, a gateway for evil forces, and the antithesis of peace by his actions.

His eyes closed, and he wept for humanity, his children, and the people of Eritria.

CHAPTER 11

MAC WOKE UP IN THE archway. Serena was sitting with her back against the wall, crying and rocking back and forth with her arms crossed in front of her. Ramos was seated with his hands crossed in his lap; Dante stood with his back toward them, his right arm raised, leaning against the rock wall. His head was down, and Mac could see it bobbing as if he were crying. Lilith was also waking, her black wings draped beneath her on the stony passage floor, and towering over all sat Xannar in a thoughtful pose, with his right hand under his solid chin. Serena began to cry louder when she saw her father awaken. "What's wrong, sweetie? We're all awake," Mas said.

"She's not," Serena said, pointing toward Jasmine, who was blacked out under a pillar.

"I'll wake her," Mac said. "Don't bother," Xannar said.

"Jasmine, wake up. It's time to go," Mac said, walking over to where she lay.

He thought she was rooted in a trance for a moment, and then he caught the dead mouse odor of rotten flesh. The closer he came, the stronger the scent became. Her body was lying unmoving in the fetal position, and now Mac was beginning to register Xannar's words.

When he touched her shoulder, the former sky captain rolled over, but she was as light as a husk of corn. Her face was shriveled like an orange left in the sun, and she had no eyes. Cobwebs filled the sockets, and as his troubled mind struggled to adjust to the horror before him, a giant black spider, disturbed by the racket, popped out of her right eye socket. Her clothes were ragged and tattered as if she had been dead for a hundred years. An instant later, she disintegrated into a gray powdery dust that blew with the gentle breeze inside Xannar's lair. "What happened to her?!" Mac said.

"Jasmine faced herself in the void and found that she could not live with what she had done. This is the result of her judgment," Xannar said.

The party was quiet, wounded, and drained.

Serena buried her face in her father's fur. "Daddy, I want this to be over," Serena said.

"Me too, sweetie, me too," Mac said, holding his daughter.

"I watched all of you sleep, and then Jasmine began to vomit blood and convulse. I tried to help, but there was nothing I could do to help her," Serena said. "She was my friend," Tears dripped down her small face.

"Jasmine killed her parents and sisters when she was a teen to satisfy the whim of a tribal leader in the overworld and gain entry into their clan. Their blood was still on her hands, and although she blocked out the memory of that tragic day, the stain was on her soul," Xannar said. "When she faced her true self, the trauma was more than her mind could bear."

"Why did the rest of us survive? I saw the horrifying images of people being liquefied, and that was a project with which I was directly involved. Dante, what happened to you in there? Ramos, what did you see?" Mac asked. "I don't want to talk about it, but apparently, I can live with the things I've done, and so can you, Mac," Ramos said.

"I crushed the skull of the last faerie on Eritria after I helped burn down their villages and kill all of the women and children. We ate them afterward to prevent any of them from regenerating," Dante said. "I'm not proud of it, but I'm not handing over my soul because of it either."

"What about you, Lilith?" Mac asked.

"I saw nothing. I saw nothing in the vision," Lilith said.

What she could have said but did not was that she saw the destruction of Earth in the future. A previously unknown planet had careened by Earth close enough to cause the planet to project away from its procession and hurtle into the far depths of space. Without the sun to warm it, the Earth turned into a dark ice ball and drifted alone into deep space.

"That's unconvincing," Ramos said.

"You saw what you saw, and I have no patience to sit around and watch you compare your experiences. Even in a life as long as mine, there are limits to where I spend my time. I'll help you on your quest," Xannar said.

"How do we get to Egypt from here?" Mac asked. I'm opening a portal through the heart of this planet that will take you from here to there, but this is no easy task," Xannar said.

"Of course not. Why?" Dante asked.

"The conduit will make you feel as if every atom in your body is being torn apart piece by piece. You'll feel the fire of torment ripping through your soul, and you will carry the experience like a scar for the rest of your lives," Xannar said.

"OK, got that, but is it safe?" Dante asked. "Relatively. You'll survive the experience intacc if that's what you mean," Xannar said.

"Well, let's get started. Bobby has no time left, and we need to figure out how to rescue him from Hell once this is over," Mac said.

"Here, take this amulet and rub it three times when you want to enter the gates. They'll appear, and you can enter, but be warned. Lucifer is no creature to be trifled with, and if you hope to survive, it will take all of your combined strength and that tablet to get your son out," Xannar said. He handed Mac a small skull-shaped bauble on a gold chain that had onyx eyes and diamond teeth that glinted in the half- light.

"Can we kill him?" Lilith asked.

"Lucifer is immortal. You can't kill him more than you can destroy space or time. However, you can get your boy out with a great enough show of force," Xannar said.

"Right, so we'll just march into Hell, the five of us, get Bobby, and march right back out," Serena said. Her tears were drying, and she stood next to her father.

"That's the plan. And by the way, this is no different than what we faced on Eritria with Asura and Broad Axe. This guy is simply better documented and more feared universally," Mac said. "We're going against a demon lord with daddy issues and an endless army of monsters to attack ant eat us. I don't see how this can fail," Lilith said.

"If you decide to enter the gates of Hell first, I will wait and transport you after your return. It's up to you,"

"Let's do it," Mac said.

"I agree to Hell with all of us," Dante said. "Your son is important, Mac. The world cad wait," Lilith said.

Mac looked at Serena. "Oh yeah, I'm in. This can't get any weirder than it already has," she said.

"I would not count on that," Mac said.

"When you're ready, commander," Lilith said and unshouldered her bow.

Mac nodded and walked to an open space in the vast passage. He rubbed the talisman between his fingers, and in a moment, they were all standing in a barren landscape in front of two massive stone doors.

"I've been here before," Mac said. His eyes went wide, and he turned back to the party. "I dreamed this,"

"Open the door, Mac," Lilith said.

He turned back, and the right door slid back, allowing the acrid odor of sulfur to fill their noses. Inside the hallway were skeletons hanging from the wall. One human skeleton was riding on the back of a rotting horse, and both were bolted to the stone with chains and spikes. The mare's skin had been stripped from her maw, giving her a permanent grin, and the eyelids were cut away, making her look completely mad.

As they entered the great hall, death greeted them, not in form, but in fashion. A chandelier of twisted wrought iron hung from the ceiling. Dangling below the fixture were iron bar cages with dead and dying people crunched up inside the confinement of their prison. One man looked down; he was old, with a long white beard, and emaciated beyond remediation.

"Gooooo back. Turn away!" He said, voice croaking. Lilith pulled back her bow and fired an energy arrow into the cage, putting the frail man out of his misery. Her shot was accurate, and in an instant, the captive's head exploded in a spray of bones, blood, and brains. She turned to Mac, who was looking at her with raised brows.

"What? He was suffering, and now he's not," Lilith said. Mac shook his head.

"Nothing. I wasn't going to say anything," Mac said. They continued down the hall, where a red light shone around a corner.

Tapestries hung from the walls, depicting great battles between white-winged angels and black- winged demons. The white angels came up from below, and the demonic forces were on high, launching their attack from the heavens. Spears, flying chariots, swords, and faces twisted with hatred on both sides added to the ominous pull of these woven works. A candelabra on a pole lit the far corner as they neared the red light.

"You said you've been here?" Dante asked. "Yeah, a few nights ago, but I thought it was n dream. I met the ferryman. I think I tossed him into the river of fire," Mac said.

They neared and then turned the corner, and just as Mac had predicted, there was a boat waiting for passengers sitting at the dock in a lake of crimson, molten rock. The ferryman was nowhere to be seen, but his oar lay on the dock alone.

"I remember pushing him into the lake and the hands of those things dragging him under. Then, I woke up on the beach, and my fur was smoking. My skin felt hot," Mac said.

"I do feel the temperature rising here, Mac. I'm not sure we can go much further if the air here gets much hotter or more poisonous," Ramos said.

"I feel fine, Daddy. I'm not hot, and the air is sweet to my nose," Serena said.

"The tablet. She's carrying the tablet," Lilith said. "Xannar did say we'd need the tablet to completa this quest," Mac said.

"Serena, please open the backpack and bring out the tablet?" Ramos asked.

"Sure, one sec," Serena said. She removed the backpack and opened the big pocket to reveal the Tablet of Destinies.

"I think we need to touch it," Lilith said. She reached out and put her finger on the tablet while the others watched.

"She's right; the air is sweet, and the heat no longer affects my skin. I feel fine," Lilith said and pulled her hand away. "I don't know how long this effect lasts, so we may want to get moving," Mac, Dante, and Ramos each touched the tablet and experienced similar results. They began to breathe freely once more as Mac led them down a red rock path toward the dock. Closer to the molten flow, they could all see the hands of the damned reaching out of the fiery liquid.

"Good job, you cleared the way for us, Mac," Dante said.

"I still can't believe I got here through a dream," Mac said. Steam and clouds of poison gas rose off the lava pool as the damned began to scream at them from their eternal bath.

"This shore may be a bad spot, but think about being one of these poor bastards," Ramos said.

"I'd rather not," Dante said.

"All aboard," Lilith said and walked to the raft. Mac followed her, picked up the oar, and hopped across to the lake transport.

The raft moved effortlessly across the lake as the hands of the faceless damned pushed them forward.

"Please, help us..." One spoke.

The entity swimming in lava formed the face of a woman Mac had known in his previous life as the commander of the unacknowledged special access projects in New Mexico. Her name was Terry Steele, a lab assistant who dealt with the initial injections of morphine and neuromuscular blocking agent for newly acquired test subjects.

"Colonel, you can get me out of here," she said.

Mac was startled and nearly fell off the raft.

Dante grabbed his arm. "Hold on a second there, Mac. Our friends in the pit of despair are playing some games with your mind, buddy. Please don't listen to it. She's not real," Dante said.

"Terry..." Mac said. He looked away, and when he turned back, her face was gone.

An entranceway to another cave appeared on the other side of the gate, but an iron gate barred it, and something moved in the dark behind it. A long, thick chain draped across the floor, but Mac could not see what was attached in the darkness.

"Oh goody, what fresh new hell is this?" Dante asked.

"There's a myth that goes back to when the Greeks ruled the world. Supposedly, a three-headed dog guards the entrance to the underworld," Mac said.

"We're wolven; a three-headed dog would have to be pretty large to scare us. Have you seen some of the creatures on our planet?" Dante asked rhetorically. They were close to the other dock now, and the chain had, so far, not moved as the black gate loomed in front of them like a skyscraper.

"They don't do things small down here, do they?" Dante asked.

"Be on your guard, brother; I sense something coming," Ramos said. He was sniffing the air.

The damned moaned and wailed in their cacophony of sorrow and misery as the living travelers above them passed by without sympathy or aid. Tormented souls forever condemned to burn, crying out against those ignoring their pain as Mac and his family of friends and daughter docked and climbed onto the rocky shore. The gate they would have to pass through was about a hundred yards from them, and the large chain began at the beach, staked into the ground with a building-sized steel bolt.

"That spike must weigh several tons," Lilith said.

"I don't feel good about this, Daddy," Serena said.

"I know, sweetie, but Bobby's in there, and this is the only way through," Mac said.

"Ramos and I need to return to Eritria when this is over. However, we can do that. We're dying on your planet, Mac. Ramos is more sensitive to it than I am, but I've been feeling somewhat...off since we crossed through that gateway," Dante said.

"I've seen my death in the desert, Mac. I'm not afraid to die, but I'd prefer it to be on Eritria, if possible," Ramos said.

"You've got it, gentlemen. I owe you a lot for what you've done for us. If there is a way, we'll make it happen," Mac said.

"Guys," Serena said. "That chain is moving," "She's right," Lilith said.

The chain dragged across the stone floor as the five readied for the unseen foe. A low growl rose from the shadows, and the party was trapped between the mystery before them and the lake of fire behind.

Ramos's eyes began to glow with eerie luminescence. Dante crouched down and readied his claws. Mac looked down at his rifle, dropped it to the ground, looked over at Dante, and grinned.

"I'm going to trust in my claws this time. Forget the rifle," Mac said.

"Good for you, Mac. You're finally starting to embrace the new you," Dante said.

"I'm leaving it right here, just in case," Mac said. "Nobody will think less of you for using it, brother," Ramos said. Orbs of spectral purple flamee circled his hands and soared high into the cavern. The purple fire spread light through the darkness, casting a psychedelic luminosity that was almost eerie, but that's when they saw the beast. "Cerberus," Mac said. He gulped at the sight of the monster before them.

Standing ten to fifteen stories above the party was a three-headed dog foaming out of each mouth.

"I think they're going to need a stronger chain," Dante said.

The demon dog had yellowish-red eyes that glared down on them like windows into a world of fire, where pain was a pleasure and pure chaos awaited anyone foolish enough to enter.

"What do we have here, mortals?" Cerberus said. He spoke with a low guttural growl from the middle head.

"Should we kill them?" asked the head to Cerberus's left.

"Only the dead pass this gate. Turn around and go back or face our wrath," The right head said.

"We're here to get my son out," Mac said.

Dante shot Mac a sideways glance, and Mac shrugged as Cerberus's heads all laughed at once. Ramos flicked his wrists, and the purple balls of flame shot forth, slamming into Cerberus's chest. The titan rocked back on his haunches but remained standing. The guardian of Hell's Gate roared with rage.

"We have to get that gate open. As long as we get beyond his chain, he can't chase us down," Dante said.

Lilith glided over to Mac and Ramos. "Mac, concentrate the fire of your rifle on the gate. Ramos, you do the same, and I'll keep the dog busy,"

"See, I knew I'd need that rifle again," Mac said. "We'll probably need every weapon we've got before this is over," Ramos said. Cerberus had stopped screaming, and in the darkness, all they could see were two large orbs of fire a city mile above their heads.

"You'll burn for your insolence!" Cerberus yelled.

"I'll burn for entirely different reasons than this!" Mac said and picked up his rifle.

He ran toward the black gates, dodging Cerberus' large feet as Lilith flew up and fired an energy arrow into the dark. It hit home, and a second later, she was tumbling to the hard ground below after Cerberus swiped at her wings and connected with a direct hit. She grunted, and Ramos lit the monster with his purple fire while Dante ran to assist Mac. The gates were locked about halfway up by a long steel chain and a padlock bigger than Mac's ranch house in Missouri.

"Let's get over there, behind the demon dog, and then we can maybe knock that lock off before he sees what we're up to," Mac said.

"I've got my bow, so both of us should be able to get it done, provided Cerberus doesn't kill the rest of our party before we finish," Dante said.

Mac had already begun firing at the lock, watching as the blue lasers bounced off while Dante followed suit with his bow, the two warriors fighting time and praying for more. Serena sensed that her father needed her and ran over to where they stood as Ramos and Lilith battled the hellhound from a distance. Cerberus's chain knocked Serena over, sending her tumbling to the ground.

She stood up and started to run again. Looking around there were no lights, but she could see her father and Dante clearly. The tablet allowed her to see in the dark. A pang of raw energy surged through her, and when she opened her mouth to scream, a blast of bright white energy exhaled from her throat.

"Serena, you're glowing," Mac said.

He stopped firing to stare at her with awe. Light emanated from her eyes and mouth, and she donned the ethereal quality of an angel. Serena walked forward slowly and swept her left hand to the side. The lock above them turned red hot and disintegrated. Chunks of iron and steel fell to the floor with a loud clang as Serena continued forward. "I'm saving my brother and leaving this place right now!" Serena said. Energy exploded from hes body, and Cerberus winced from sudden exposure. "Stop it! Make it go away! You can pass!"

Cerberus said. He was mewling, groaning.

"Too late!" Serena said, waving her right arm his way. "You should have been friendlier,"

Serena turned toward Cerberus and crossed her arms as she lunged forward. Then, she threw a force blast so powerful that Cerberus slammed against the cavern wall, and all three heads were knocked unconscious.

Cerberus hit the ground with an audible thump, and the gate creaked open on hinges older than time. Everyone looked at one another in silence as her glow subsided.

"OK, are we ready? Let's go," Serena said.

"You heard the lady? Let's get on with it," Ramos said.

"How'd you know you could do that?" Dante asked.

"I didn't. I was standing there freaking out when a flash went off in my head, and then I felt something pushing me forward. After that, I turned into a light bulb and found I was able to move things around with my mind,"

"That's very impressive, young lady. Let's get your brother before that thing wakes up, and we have to deal with him again," Mac said.

"Right, Dad," Serena said.

They walked into darkness with nothing but Dante's light guided them, and they exited the tunnel into a nightscape across an odd twilight jungle landscape. Low-lying plants grew in the half- darkness, with significant lava fields several hundred yards away.

"This is what the hell looks like?" Mac asked. "This is only the upstairs, Mac. Nine levels belor us are filled with the tormented souls of those who put themselves down here," Lilith said.

"What do you mean?" Mac asked.

"We all have the power to choose where we want to go, how we want to live our lives, and what our mind will accept as truth. The souls down here accepted Hell as truth long before their deaths, and in doing so, they created their own," Lilith said. "The people in Hell are here because they want to be?" Mac asked.

"Essentially, yes. They all have the power to release themselves from their self-imposed punishment for wrongdoing that is very much subjective in the multiverse," Lilith said.

"How do you know all of this?" Mac asked. "I've been around for over a few years, sweetie,"

Lilith said.

A tall, dark castle loomed in the distance.

"Did you see where Bobby landed when he went through the portal?" Mac asked.

"It was a barren wasteland of fire and smoke; that's all I saw before Azazel closed the portal," Dante said.

Ramos looked to the left, and beyond the jungle was a landscape that fit Dante's recollection.

"Let's go that way. I think I see a building, but it's very dark. My eyesight doesn't work as well in this darkness.

It's almost like the absence of light rather than normal nighttime in this place," Ramos said.

"I noticed the same thing, brother," Dante said. Mac led them over to the left, where their feet eventually left the rich, dark jungle landscape and touched a surface that was more like the moon on fire. A building did exist where Ramos had said it did, and it looked to Mac like a maintenance shew constructed of cinderblocks with a steel roof. "This looks out of place," Mac said. "There's a door with a lock on it," Lilith said. Mac fired his rifle and heard an audible clink as the internal lock broke. It swung wide on rusty steel hinges and made a grinding, groaning sound. "Heeeeeeeelp!" A voice from behind the door said.

"Bobby!" Mac said. He moved forward, and Dante grabbed his arm.

"Careful, it might be a trap," Dante said. "This whole place is a trap," Mac said.

"Yeah, but your old pal from back on that beach is waiting for you to come get your boy," Dante said.

"True," Mac said. With his rifle raised, he crept through the door and saw a spiral set of stairs carved from the rock wall leading down into oblivion.

"Watch your step, Daddy," Serena said. "Heeeelp!" The voice cried again.

"Coming little buddy, hang in there," Mac whispered.

Down, down, down, the two-foot-wide staircase wound in a dizzyingly tight spiral that threatened to give them all vertigo. There was no handrail; one false slip would send any of them tumbling into a red eye of molten lava below. A ghostly figure rushed up through the stairwell, racing through the center of the well, screaming and wailing like a banshee. It was translucent white and wore the screaming face of a terrified human.

Mac stepped back into the wall and almost slipped as it flew by him. Two more followed the first. Four more came. Each one was wearing a mask of terror, and the last one looked into Mac's eyes with the hollow expression of the grave. Those black sockets peered into his soul, and then the spirit disappeared. "It looks like we found the Well of Souls," Lilith said.

"Whatever it is, I'll be glad when we're at the bottom," Dante said.

"I'll be glad when we rescue Bobby and get out of here," Serena said.

"Do you think the owner knows we're invading his home?" Ramos asked.

Lilith felt an alarm go off in her mind. "Don't speak his name, not while we're in this realm," Lilith said.

Mac felt the hair standing up on his neck at Lilith's warning. The childhood stories of speaking the devil's name and his appearance came flooding back. Mac saw an opening further down and a shadow cast on the stairwell.

"Looks like we've got something different coming up," Mac said.

"Different, good?" Dante asked. Mac shrugged.

A few moments later, they entered a cavern within the well. It was tall, broad, and looked like it had been carved out of solid red rock. A cage was swinging from the ceiling, and a black figure sat inside, looking out at the host of characters entering from below.

"Dad?" Bobby asked. His black hybrid demon and wolven face were stuck between the bars as he strained to get a better look.

"We've come to get you, son!" Mac said.

He felt rage coursing through him at the thought of his little boy being stuck in a cage, and a low guttural growl emanated from deep within his throat. As if on cue, Azazel appeared between Mac and his son.

"Welcome to Hell, Colonel! I've been waiting for you. Prepare to meet my master and die!" Azazel said.

"Harper, get bent," Mac said.

He raised his rifle with one arm while staring up at his son in the cage, and then he aimed it at Azazel and squeezed the trigger. A single blue bolt left his weapon and zipped through the air with lightning speed.

"Your weapons cannot harm me, Colonel..." Harper said. That was all he was able to tell before a dark hole opened in his forehead, and the disciple of Lucifer fell forward, landing on his face.

"I guess he was mortal after all," Ramos said. "Yeah, and so are we. Let's get out of here beford that guy's boss realizes we're here," Lilith said.

The ground beneath their feet trembled as if an Earthquake were coming.

"I think we need to go. Right now," Ramos said. Lilith flew up and tore open the cage holding Bobby. He fell into her arms, weak from torture and malnourished. She landed with Bobby and laid hie on the ground.

"Can you carry Serena and Bobby?" Mac asked. "I'm sorry, Bobby's too heavy. I can carry one or the other, but not both," Lilith said.

"Get Bobby out of here, and we'll be right behind you," Mac said.

The sound of a million demons rumbling the ground like thunder and, if possible, escape would be tight. Lilith picked the teenage demon up and whisked him away through the Well of Souls as Mac, Serena, and the two wolven brothers made a dash for the stairs. It would be a long run back to the entrance, and Hell was on their heels.

CHAPTER 12

LILITH SOARED UP THROUGH THE Well of Souls holding Bobby in her arms, her wings beating the thin, hot air ferocity as she sought to get him to safety. In the distance, she could see dust rising across the dark, reddish-black horizon and she could hear the battle cries of the demon hordes. Lilith flew through the jungle, back into the tunnel they had entered, and nearly made it to the lake of fire when she confronted a conscious and aware Cerberus lying before the gate, right paw crossed over left. He appeared to be grinning at her. A cold shiver ran up her spine as she held the boy in her arms and confronted Hell's guardian.

"Are you going to fight me?" Lilith asked. Cerberus laughed and chuffed a cloud of sulfurous smoke into the air. "No, I have no more quarrels with you, pretty lady. What you've done will soon seal your fate, and then I can get back to my nap," Cerberus said. The center head was talking while the other two looked at her with, what was it? Pity?

"What do you mean?" Lilith asked.

"You entered the forbidden doorway, killed an executive demon, and stole a prisoner from Lucifer. Did you think there wouldn't be a price to pay for that? What did you think that the devil fights fairly? He'll eat your soul and spit it out onto the doorway of heaven."

Lilith suddenly had a premonition that while she was almost free, her friends might not make it. "If I leave him here, will no harm come to him?" Lilith asked.

"Not by me, my lady," Cerberus yawned. "I'd hurry, though; your time is short." A clock appeared next to his head, and the hands began spinning. They cycled around the clock face until each hand malfunctioned and bounced off the face on springs. Lilith laid Bobby on the ground and darted back through the tunnel with desperation, flying past the jungle until she saw Mac and Serena coming up out of the well. Souls were gushing from the depths and soaring into the blackening sky above, translucent horrors from the depths of a prison world called forth by their dark master to seek vengeance upon the interlopers.

Mac and Serena ran toward the jungle as Dante and Ramos surfaced. The wolven brothers were running faster than Lilith had ever seen them travel. Ramos stood at the edge of the well, firing a volley of purple fire down the hole. Chunks of stone erupted into the air, floating in space as if suspended by invisible strings. Mac lifted

Serena from her feet and carried her while Dante and Ramos joined in the escape. Dust kicked up behind them while the horde of demons closed in on the party. Lilith flew down and snatched Serena from her father as Serena began to scream her father's name.

"It'll be alright, Serena. Go with Lilith," Mac said.

Lilith was gone in a flash, along with his little girl. Closer now, the jungle was only paces ahead, and as Ramos looked back, he could see the first of the demons approaching. The leading pack was close to twenty dog-faced monstrosities with hunchbacks and lesions covering their bodies. They looked like stitched-together horror dolls, and Ramos did not want to find out how they smelled up close.

They cleared the jungle and bolted through the tunnel as the sounds behind them grew louder. Cerberus waved a paw as they entered his chamber, and although Mac was confused that Cerberus was allowing them to pass, he had no time to question it.

"The raft!" Lilith yelled.

Bobby and Serena were already aboard, and as the first of the ghouls arrived, she laid down cover fire with red-orange fire from her hands. Lilith gave the boys the time to make the distance between the tunnel's opening and the raft. All were aboard when the first volley of arrows whizzed through the air, narrowly missing Ramos as an arrow pierced through his robe and landed in the lava. Mac returned fire from his rifle, and Dante did the same with the energy bow. Lilith was still floating above them, riding the thermals, and blasting their enemies below as she followed the raft across the river of molten death.

"Ramos, you've got dominion over the dead; can you command these poor bastards to fight for you?" Mac asked.

"I don't know. I've only controlled bodies, but these are souls," Ramos said. His eyes glowed purple, and large orbs spun around his head just before launching into a pack of demons.

"Try, my friend," Mac said.

Ramos turned his palms upward and spread his hands to the side while concentrating on the millions of lost souls burning below their feet. He heard their cries of pain and anger and promised them vengeance if they rose to fight for him. Telepathy with the dead was a great trick, but getting them to listen to him outside of their torment proved more difficult than he imagined.

"Come on! Get up and fight!" Ramos screamed. Strings of purple light exploded from his hands like a taffy machine gone haywire, and against all logic, the trapped souls rose from their eternal imprisonment. The cursed souls rose from the lava and gained their previous physical forms. Humans, minotaur, wolven, elves, mole men, greys, insectoids, reptilians, an army of the dead courtesy of Ramos, and each of them turned to face their new master.

"Tear their faces off and throw them into your lake of fire!" Ramos said.

The new army erupted with a great battle cry, and they attacked the demon horde. In seconds, screams and weapons clanging together filled the cavern. Cerberus, content to watch, crushed a demon or two as they passed. When the raft arrived at the dock, Cerberus waved a paw at Mac and his friends and then turned his attention back to the battle.

"Why do I feel like we almost just died?" Dante said. "Because we did. Let's go; those risen spirits won't stay that way forever," Ramos said.

"Agreed, that was way too close!" Mac said. "Bobby, are you alright?"

"I don't think I can control myself much longer, Dad, but other than that, yeah, I'm doing fine," Bobby said.

"I think we can get you fixed, but we have to get back to Xannar first," Mac said.

"Who or what is that? No, wait, never mind," Bobby said.

He had midnight black fur, and his horns were growing more pronounced. Bobby's maw was shorter than the wolven's, but he was just as muscular, and after exposure to the tablet, his strength returned almost immediately.

"There's the opening!" Serena said. "The doorway, let's go!" Lilith said.

They raced toward the door and closed it behind them, listening as the giant steel barrier clanged shut.

"That won't keep them contained," Xannar said.

He was perched atop a cliff above them. "What?" Mac asked.

"You've unleashed the forces of Hell upon you. You'd better hope the tablet can restore this planet, or you'll be looking at a hot reception in Egypt. I believe Lucifer is aware of your presence now," Xannar said.

He'll be looking for a replacement for Azazel, Colonel," Xannar said.

"What, one of us?" Mac asked.

"No, most likely you. The amulet, please?" Xannar said. Mac turned the talisman over to Xannar and felt his stomach croak.

"They're also coming for me, aren't they?" Bobby said.

"Not if you are fleet of foot and right my world right again, Colonel. I believe you said you needed to go to Egypt?" Xannar said.

"That's right Xannar, as fast as possible. I believe there is a warrior tribe there that can help us finish the job," Mac said.

Xannar briefly nodded and closed his hard eyes before waving his hands around in a circle, his fingers emitting a green light. Ornate runes filled the ring, moving in three dimensions, becoming a sphere, and in the center of the sorcerer's orb, an all-seeing eye formed. The orb grew larger until it was large, then wolven-sized, and finally, the eye started to show light through it, like a small star.

The demons were at the door now, smashing through it like a fist on a saltine. Xannar looked into the orb and closed his eyes again, humming a small, melodic tune. As the vibration of his song reacted with the sphere, a bright circle formed within. At first, it was tiny, no more than a speck, and then the size of a dinner plate. At last, they could see a pyramid in the distance and what was left of the Sphinx as she stood against a mountain of sand.

"Please step through the gate before my concentration wanes," Xannar said, continuing to hum.

"Bobby, Serena, you go first," Mac said. "Let's go together," Serena said, taking hem father and brother's hands.

They stepped through Xannar's portal onto a barren desert landscape in the dead heat of an Egyptian summer. Lilith followed, followed by Dante and Ramos.

"This land was cursed long ago. I see a thriving society in my mind's eye, wiped out by a major Earthly disturbance. There were once rivers and forests where there is sand," Ramos said.

"He's right. The last time I was here, the land was lush, and rivers flowed through, feeding crops as far as the eye could see. It's so...desolate now," Lilith said.

"Yeah, well, welcome to the twenty-third century.

It's a hot, barren place," Mac said. The gate was still open behind them, and Mac could hear the monsters coming.

"Oh, and Colonel," Xannar said. "Yes?" Mac said.

Xannar's massive head peered at him through the portal. "If you don't get this right, I'm holding you personally responsible for the trouble, and you won't have to worry about Lucifer anymore. I'll imprison your soul in a little jar and keep it on my shelf in the chaos dimension,"

"Thanks for the vote of confidence; I won't let you down," Mac said. He gulped hard as Xannar gave him one last flat stare, grimacing, and then the portal shut.

"One thing I never considered before deciding to come this way was water," Mac said.

"Right, we don't have any," Bobby said.

"Maybe they do," Ramos said. He pointed to three figures on horseback riding toward them at a gallop.

"Who do you suppose that is?" Serena asked. "Help, hopefully," Mac said.

"They don't appear to have horns, so we can assume they're not demons. That's right, right?" Dante said. "This place has gone so far south; I don't think we can assume anything anymore. Get ready to fight these guys if they try anything," Mac said.

"Hey, what do you suppose is going through their minds, seeing a bunch of wolf men, a little girl, and a winged hottie standing in the desert?" Bobby asked.

"Good point. Stay focused and be ready for anything," Mac said.

"What's the signal?" Bobby asked. "What?" Mac asked.

"The signal to strike if things look like they're going bad," Bobby said.

"Oh, um, how about...I never did mind about the little things. I saw that in a movie once." Mac shrugged.

"Charming," Ramos said.

"Kind of rolls off the tongue, doesn't it," Mac said.

"Here they come," Lilith said.

The men on horseback were garbed in linen robes wrapped around their bodies with hoods that obscured any facial features. One rode a black horse, and the other two sat atop brown stallions. They slowed from a gallop to a walk as the rider of the black horse broke from the pack and trotted over to the party. He slowed and looked down, removing the hood from his head. The man was black with deep lines crisscrossing his face from a hundred years of beating, blinding sun. The hair on his head was white like snow, and he had cataracts across his eyes that made them appear milky and grayish. For a moment, he sat staring at the strangers.

"Who is the leader of your group?" He spoke.

Everyone looked at Mac.

"That would be me. I'm Colonel MacDonald, call me Mac," Mac said.

"My name is Tbilisi, and the two behind me are my sons, Yorag and Rohim. Are you a wolf, man? " The man said. He had an audible African accent when he spoke.

"It's a long story, but no, I'm not a wolf man, still human when I want to be. We are in a hurry though and..." Mac said.

"You're here to repair the global energy grid and send the demons back to their dimensions," Tbilisi said.

"Yes, but how did you know?" Mac asked.

"One night around the fire, I asked for guidance from the great spirit, and it revealed an image of you people," Tbilisi said.

"What do you mean, you people?" Dante asked. "Us?" Mac asked. "You were entering from another world, and you had an artifact of great power with you," Tbilisi said. He looked over at Serena. "The child has it,"

"How do you know that, sir? Can you see it?" Serena asked.

"Hah, I have not seen anything in over thirty years. Now, what exactly is your mission? My vision did not extend that far," Tbilisi asked. His men were armed with long rifles, but they were holstered alongside their horses, and none of the men seemed hostile toward the party.

"We've got the Tablet of Destinies, and a vision told me to bring it to the Great Pyramid. We came here to place it inside, I think. In the dream, or whatever it was, I was on a wooden ship with my friends and the tablet," Mac said.

"I believe you should come with us. There is something I want you to see but beware of the sandworms; they have been highly active lately," Tbilisi said.

"Sandworms, what?" Mac asked. "We must go," Tbilisi said.

Mac turned around to see the Great Pyramid rising high into the sky, and with her granite casing, the stones replaced in the structure looked brand new. All three pyramids had been restored to their former glory, giving them a regal presence amid the desolation of the desert. Mac felt a tugging in his soul to get the tablet inside the largest of the three, but first, he needed something else: the catalyst. Then he remembered the box he had seen the men carrying in his dream.

"Mac, we will return to complete your task. I think yours and ours are the same mission. Now please, follow me," Tbilisi said.

Tbilisi removed a small gun from his robe with a large bore barrel and pointed it at the eastern sky. Tbilisi fired a flare and waited a moment, and then dust began to rise over the horizon.

"He seems to see an amazing amount for a man with cataracts covering his eyes," Dante said.

"I can fix him if he wishes. Gregor showed me how to use an ocular regeneration spell," Ramos said.

"Yeah, but his books are on the other side of the galaxy," Dante said.

"I memorized it," Ramos said.

"Why? Of all the spells our father had in those tomes?" Dante said.

"You never know when you're going to need something like that, and it seems like now is an opportune time for such a use," Ramos said.

"You're a complicated man," Dante said. Ramos nodded his head. "I know." As the dust cloud rose and grew closer, Mac could hear the familiar sound of mechanized vehicles. Tbilisi and his men watched the cloud move forward with stoic expressions on their faces. "You have vehicles? But...how?" Mac asked.

Tbilisi never took his eyes off the approaching sand cloud.

"The better question is, why were you preparing us to run all the way back to wherever you came from?" Bobby asked.

"Hah, I was having some fun with you, my friend. We have not had other people come out this way in an extraordinarily long time," Tbilisi said.

Mac chuckled. "Good one. So, how did you get your hands on vehicles made more than a hundred and fifty years ago?" Mac asked.

"One of my sons was walking in the desert when he found a metal door sticking out of the sand. He is fearless, you see, and he opened it to see what was inside, and he found a long stairwell leading down into darkness," Tbilisi said.

"You found a bunker," Mac said. It was more of a whisper to himself than a statement for Tbilisi. The man continued to speak.

"He ran back to the town and informed the elders. We could not believe what our eyes showed us when we descended the stairs. It was a huge metal room, so wide and long that it took us three days to walk around it. What we found were these vehicles, rifles, rockets, land mines, tanks, and a few bombs that had been left there by whoever had come before us," Tbilisi said.

"You found an armory underground," Mac said. "Yes! While it took us a little time to understanr how to use all of it, these vehicles have helped us rebuild our tribe," Tbilisi said.

"Everything was preserved?" Mac asked.

"Yes, by this very oily substance that covered all of the metal parts," Tbilisi said.

"Cosmoline coating. They covered it all with cosmoline," Mac said.

A giant green deuce and a half rolled up next to them, its engine rumbling at idle, reminding Mac of his former days as a commander of an installation in the military. Those were days long gone, but here in the middle of the desert, a hundred and fifty years later, was a fleet of vehicles that should have been nothing but rusted-out hulks of scrap metal.

"You've got a troop transport. What about a fuel depot?" Mac asked.

"Come, my friends. Time is short and getting shorter every minute. We have much to discuss," Tbilisi said. "Do you have any Tesla towers near you out here?" Mac asked.

"We have not had them around us for over a hundred years. Too many monsters came through in the old days, which was unbelievably bad for our people, and although our tribe was almost destroyed in the attempt, we managed to eliminate their access to our little part of the world."

The deuce and a half rumbled to life as the driver put it in gear and stood on the brake and clutch.

" Babatunde is growing impatient, and the sandworms are worse at night. It's not as hot for them," Tbilisi said.

"Let's go then," Mac said, and the party climbed into the back of the giant truck.

In moments, they all sat inside the open-roof rear of the M35A2 two-and-a-half-ton transport and felt the rumble under their rear ends as the vehicle moved forward. It was the first time any of them had rested in days.

"We need sleep," Mac said.

"Yeah, you guys all look like crap," Dante said. "You're not looking so good yourself, brother; you've got bags under your eyes so large that I could pack half of Gregor's books in them," Ramos said.

"You might be right, come to think of it," Dante said. He yawned as he gazed at the setting sun. The small convoy raced across the sand toward the town as Tbilisi rode his horse beside the deuce and a half. Mac sat with his head down, looking at the floor, feeling every muscle ache as he longed for a night of sleep, listening to his belly growl for food. So far, none of the tribe members had raised the alarm at having a winged sorceress, a teenage girl, and four wolf men with them. As choking dust rose from the arid desert floor, the sun appeared like a giant orange ball in the cloudless sky.

"We will be there soon, and we shall have a huge feast," Tbilisi said. He looked at them all smiling, his milky white eyes gleaming.

"That sounds good to me!" Mac said and yawned. "You will have a good night's rest, and we cad begin in the morning," Tbilisi said.

The world turned upside down in the next instant as a massive jolt slammed them onto the floor, and then everyone in the back of the deuce tumbled through the air like balls inside a popper machine. Mac landed hard on his back, skidding across the ground; Serena fell into him while Bobby and Ramos collided in mid-air.

Dante saw what hit them a second before impact and sprung off the truck just in time to avoid catastrophe. He performed a forward flip and landed on the ground, skidding on his feet, and supporting his balance with his two powerful arms. Dante slowed himself with his razor-sharp claws, and while his friends and family were tossed like toys across the desert, he righted himself for combat.

In front of him, coursing through the sand, was a cylindrical nightmare of teeth and flesh.

"So, you're a sandworm," Dante told the beast.

He was tired, and his irritation was quickly turning into anger. He growled, bared his teeth, and prepared to launch at the monster before him. The worm was approximately twice the height of the deuce and a half and looked like an Earthworm escaping from a mad science lab. The worm had multiple rows of teeth that appeared to be rotating like a grinder inside its formidable mouth. It was only feet from him as he dived to the side, performed a somersault out of the way, and then a backflip onto the worm's back. He landed and dug his toe claws into the worm, looking down to see a fresh wound in his right forearm where one of the teeth had caught him during his evasive maneuver. The worm was heading directly for Serena as it attempted to buck Dante off.

"Oh no, you don't!" Dante said.

He used the claws on his hands to dig into the harsh, leathery skin of the sandworm's head. Using all of his strength, he guided the worm away from Serena ran toward the overturned truck while she got to her feet. Dante howled and dug in deeper, trying to figure out his next move. Ramos saw Dante riding the sandworm and rushed to get in front of them with lightning reflexes and speed.

"It's about time you helped out!" Dante said. "You seemed to have everything under control. n didn't want to step on your toes," Ramos said.

He spread his hands apart as an arch of purple energy filled the gap, and as Dante rode the sandworm directly toward his brother, Ramos formed a giant ball. With its mouth open wide, teeth rotating within, hungrily grinding the air in search of food, the simple-minded monster bucked Dante and ran into oblivion.

"Be gone, foul beast!" Ramos said.

The worm received a final meal of purple flames while Dante leaped from it with the grace of a ninja, landing on his feet beside Ramos. Ramos's spell worked its magic inside the worm, searing the internal organs, burning its heart, and erupting blood vessels. It stopped moving, and the fire consumed the worm from within its body, sending black rivulets of smoke from the mouth. The internal pressure caused the flesh to burst into tiny pieces.

"Aw! It smells like garbage on fire," Bobby said.

He was placing his hand in front of his nose. "Yeah, not a great odor, but we're all still alive.

Thank you for saving my daughter, Dante. You too, Ramos," Mac said.

"The driver is dead, and we have to get moving before more worms arrive," Tbilisi said.

The deuce and a half were overturned on the driver's side. Tbilisi's man had been trapped under it as the vehicle was rocked onto its side. His twisted, broken body lay half-crushed under the roof, an expression of terror frozen on his dead face. He looked like a man who had died staring into the reality of cosmic abyssal horrors.

"I can drive," Mac said. "Let's get this thing turned right side up and get out of here,"

Without another word, the wolven brothers walked over and helped Bobby and Lilith set the truck on all four wheels again. Mac pulled their driver's crushed body from underneath the vehicle, giving Tbilisi a look, hoping the old man could see something or at least give him further instructions on what to do with it.

"Leave our brother here for the desert to consume him once more. We are created from the Earth, and to it, we shall return when life is over," Tbilisi said. "You got it," Mac said and laid the body dowI away from their vehicle. "You heard the man, let's get going. More of those things are coming, and I don't want to be here when they do," Mac said.

The party reassembled inside the back of the deuce, and Mac fired up the engine. It roared to life again after a few false starts, and he engaged the clutch. They were rolling a moment later, and now Mac could see a city in the distance. Twenty minutes later, they were motoring through what used to be a massive industrial city where thousands of people were lining the streets to see the newcomers: the strangers of renown who had come to help them restore balance.

Mac drove slowly through the lane as the desert dwellers covered their faces and heads to protect themselves from blowing dust and the sun's harsh, beating rays. Tbilisi rode alongside Mac momentarily, shouting above the engine's roar.

"Pull up to the large gray building two blocks from here. That is the community center where we will eat. Then, you sleep, and tomorrow, we can sort the rest of this out," Tbilisi said.

Mac drove on, and once he parked, they got out of the deuce, happy to be on solid ground again. They were standing on a torn-up and neglected sidewalk in front of the building, with a sign above it that read *bēte mets'aḥifiti* in Amharic, which Tbilisi translated for them as a library. "Looks like we're here," Mac said.

"Come upstairs, my friends. Let's eat," Tbilisi said.

They followed him up the stairs and into a large banquet hall, where people were already eating soup with a brownish-black broth. Tbilisi showed them to their seats, and a moment later, a man walked over and ladled some of the soup into their bowls.

"What's this?" Serena asked.

"Don't be rude, Serena," Mac said. His furry brows were raised.

"I was just asking what it was, not commenting on the validity of it as an edible food source," Serena said. She rolled her eyes and sniffed the broth. Satisfied it was not poison, she slurped some off her spoon.

"Calf brain stew," Tbilisi said, smiling.

Serena wrinkled her nose, but she knew that stopping eating could be an insult to Tbilisi and his tribe.

"I could have gone the rest of my life not knowing that," Serena said.

"Mmmmm, just like Gregor used to make," Dante said.

"This is quite delicious, Tbilisi. Thank you for your hospitality; it is much appreciated," Mac said. "Thank you for killing that sandworm. That was quite a stunt and quickly orchestrated," Tbilisi said. "Tbilisi, I was wondering if I might have a worn with you," Ramos said.

"Speak freely. We're all friends now," Tbilisi said. "How would you like to have your vision back?"

Ramos said.

The old man chuckled and nodded his head. "I would like that very much. I would also like nine wives, but sadly, I am stuck with only three."

"I can repair your vision if you allow me," Ramos said.

Tbilisi considered this for a moment. "Does this require any knives near my eyeballs? Because if it does, my answer is no," Tbilisi said.

"No knives and twenty minutes of your time," Ramos said.

"OK, then. When do you want to do it?" Tbilisi asked.

"How soon is it now? You can sit here while I perform the incantation," Ramos said.

Tbilisi nodded approval, and Ramos entered a trance, speaking in a language unfamiliar to even Dante. The vibratory energy of Ramos' words caused the table to shake, and then Tbilisi was taken by the spell. His back arched, his chin pointed toward the ceiling, and his arms stiffened out to his side as if he were being electrocuted.

Some of Tbilisi's men raised their rifles toward Ramos but made no other move in case breaking the spell would hurt their leader. Tbilisi remained like this for several minutes, eyes open wide, mouth agape, frozen in Ramos's magical incantation as the white, milky substance across his eyes faded. Finally, it was over, and Ramos released his grip on the tribal leader. Tbilisi slowly relaxed and closed his eyes. When he opened them again, tears of joy streamed down his cheeks.

"I can see. I can see! Thank you very much, Ramos. I do not know how to repay you, but I am forever in your debt," Tbilisi said.

Tbilisi's henchmen lowered their weapons, smiling. By the end of that evening, the rumor spread throughout the entire city that saviors from the other world were here to help them. All were given separate rooms within the ancient library, now a fortress, to sleep for the night. Tbilisi bid them all good night before adjourning himself, but it would be hours before he could fall asleep as he sat staring up at the billions of stars twinkling down on him. He feared that he would go to sleep and wake up blind again, but around midnight, he drifted off to a dream-filled slumber. His dream showed him and his men following the travelers from far away, and in their hands, supported on long wooden poles, was the Ark of the Covenant.

Tbilisi watched the Ark disappear into the Great Pyramid accompanied by the magical tablet the strangers had brought. His dreaming mind sensed the presence of a power not yet seen in these parts, something evil, a vile entity bent on their destruction. Before he sat up in bed, drenched in sweat, he stared into the faceless glowing eyes of an ageless horror. The demon laughed at him, and his gleaming black horns reflected the light of a sun half-covered by a lunar eclipse. For the first time since he had begun dreaming of the stranger's arrival, Tbilisi started to feel very afraid.

CHAPTER 13

MAC FELL INTO THE DREAM once more, standing before the Great Pyramid. But this time, it was different; his vision was global. He saw every ancient megalith ever created in the old world and felt a connectedness between them. His mind raced from Giza to Stonehenge, and then Angkor Wat, Mohenjo Daro, and then Nazca, and on to Easter Island. The wind blew, and sand whirled around in eddies as he stood looking up into a clear blue sky where the sun and moon were both beaming brightly and adjacent in the middle of the day. The next moment, the moon moved between the Earth and the sun, creating a total eclipse, and darkening the sky.

In his hands was the Tablet of Destinies and the hope of humanity; by his foot was an ornately carved box with two angelic gold statues facing each other about a foot apart. Their wings were set back, and their arms were outstretched as if they were reaching to embrace each other. He held the tablet near the angels and watched them spark to life as an arc of electricity spanned the distance between them. While Mac watched dreamily, the angels stopped generating electricity, turned toward him, and pointed to the tablet in his hands. Mac woke up and stared at the ceiling, exhausted from the journey and ready to take an extended vacation. So much has happened in the past year. He wondered whether anything would be normal again or if it was too late to return. Mac reflected on a fishing trip he and Bobby had taken years ago and how quiet it had been on that lake, just the two of them, father, and son. That was one of the most peaceful days he had experienced in a long time, and he longed to return to that day.

"Get up, get moving. You're not done yet," Mac said to himself.

He threw his legs over the bed, careful not to wake Lilith, who was deep in sleep and snoring. He studied her wings, which, to him, were beautiful and carried her on the wind like a fallen angel. Lilith lay turned with her back toward him, and he could see her rippling muscles gently rising and falling as she breathed. But now Lilith was gone, and in her place, horror struck him like the chime of a doomsday clock as he looked into a dark, male face with evil yellow eyes glaring back at him.

Two long horns sprouted from the monster's head, and the ears became pointed and elfish, and Mac became terrified. She became the demon lord instantly, and he realized that Lucifer had found him. As he struggled to escape, Mac could feel his skin burning, the fat catching fire and melting onto the bed. He turned to run, but there was no escape. Lucifer rose from the bed, and his black dragon wings spread across the window, blotting out the sunlight.

"No! No! Please, God help me!" Mac said.

He was screaming, and his eyes were on fire, but the scene shifted, and he stood before the gate from his nightmare; only now, flowers bloomed around the entrance, and he could see more green grass than before. Carol was there, her arms outstretched on the other side, beckoning for him. She smiled with a warmth he thought no longer existed in his universe, and as he ran for her, his feet succumbed to the flames, and the pain drove him to his knees.

He crawled, burning alive, toward the open gate as Lucifer appeared, blocking his egress to freedom. Mac looked up again into the beast's eyes and snapped awake in bed.

He was drenched in sweat, crying out as he sat up, claws bared, his pillow torn apart, snarling in wolven form and afraid.

"My God," Mac said and got out of bed.

He walked through the ancient, majestic, granite hallways until he saw Tbilisi walking toward him with a grave expression. Mac became concerned as his mind repeatedly played the dream in an endless loop of terror. "Good morning, Mac. Could you come with me?

There's something I must show you," Tbilisi said. "OK, what is it?" Mac asked.

"It would be better if you saw," Tbilisi said, guiding Mac to a stairwell leading down. "How did you sleep?"

"Rough. My dreams are all dark lately. Guess I need to get more than eight hours of sleep in a week, huh?" Mac said.

"Were you on fire?" Tbilisi asked.

"Yes, actually, I was. But wait, how did you...?" Mac asked.

"Because I had the same dream. In it, I was standing outside the Great Pyramid, but Lucifer appeared and set me ablaze as I tried to walk inside," Tbilisi said.

Mac's mouth opened wide. What kind of madness were they dealing with? He wondered. They walked down the stairwell and then across a breezeway to another set of stairs leading further into the dark. Tbilisi paused and looked over his shoulder to ensure no one was following them, and then they descended into a cave below the library. Winding through one tunnel after another, they encountered armed guards sporting automatic weapons with their faces covered. "I'm afraid we are running out of time. The deceiver will be here soon," Tbilisi said.

"Where are you taking me, Tbilisi?" Mac asked. "We are going to retrieve an artifact of great power that my people have guarded with their lives for over two thousand years. It was preserved for a day like this when the lives of men are threatened with extinction," Tbilisi said.

They walked for ten minutes before stopping at a thick wooden door blocking the way, guarded by two men with rifles. One of them wore a bandolier filled with hand grenades.

"What's with all the firepower down here?" Mac asked.

"If our enemies knew what we had down here, they would come for it and try to use it against us. We are warrior priests guarding mankind's greatest secret," Tbilisi said.

The guards made no move against them, only exchanged uneasy glances with each other. Tbilisi knocked on the door in a rhythmic, coded pattern, and it opened on creaking hinges. Mac's nostrils became overpowered by the smell of death from within the dark room. He saw a figure seated before a wooden box with his night vision.

"Forgive the odor. This room has seen many watchers," Tbilisi said. "Why is a man sitting in here, and why does it smell like rotten meat?" Mac asked.

"Our people watch over the Ark and make sure that no one unworthy enters this room. If we were not in such a crisis, your head could be hacked off for even laying eyes on the artifact. As for the odor, the Ark has power to it, and mortal man cannot be near for long and survive. Seven years is the longest any of us has ever spent with it. The energy inside is so powerful that it tears flesh from bone and rots a man from within. The cataracts

Ramos removed from me were a result of exposure to the Ark when I was a younger man," Tbilisi said.

"Tbilisi, is that you?" A man asked. His voice was cracked and old.

"Yes, Mutombo. I have a friend with me, and we have come to take the Ark to her final resting place," Tbilisi said.

"So, it is time, and I am the last caretaker. Thank God above," Mutombo said.

"Yes, and we need to move quickly. The demon lord is rising, and we have to end his mischief before the final war can begin," Tbilisi said.

"Final war?" Mac asked.

"Lucifer has been planning this since he fell out of grace with his father. The watchers of God banished him to the underworld where he has been planning to destroy the favored creation of the architects: humanity," Tbilisi said.

"You know what to do, Tbilisi. Take the Ark and save our people," Mutombo said.

Tbilisi moved with speed in the darkness while Mac watched him, and in a moment, he returned with two long poles. Tbilisi slid them through two sets of metal rings near the top of the Ark, and when he did, the two shooters from outside the door entered the room, each of them taking a pole while Mac grabbed the pole on the back, and they all lifted in unison.

"This thing is a lot lighter than I thought it would be," Mac said.

"Just wait until we get it outside. The Ark levitates," Tbilisi said.

"I read that this device was at the wall of Jericho, just before the walls were crushed to dust when the horn was blown," Mac said.

"The Ark is a hazardous and powerful weapon, and that is why my people took it from Jerusalem and hid it for so long. The people of that region would have used it against each other and not for its intended purpose: enlightenment in dark times. It's a spiritual weapon, Mac, and a great responsibility," Tbilisi said. Mac thought Tbilisi's Ethiopian accent made him seem like one of the wise men from a movie about the apocalypse. Tired and worn out, the Colonel found it exhilarating that he was holding a pole that supported the legendary Ark of the Covenant.

They walked through the tunnels back to the stairwell. Mac followed Tbilisi down to the surface, where hordes of people gathered to see the Ark revealed for the first time in their lives. Serena stood with Lilith and Dante as they came out of the catacombs beneath the city.

"Dad! Where were you? We were looking everywhere," Serena said, and as the Ark got closer, she began emanating white light like an aura around her body. "Oh my gosh! What's happening to me? Not again!"

"The tablet in your backpack is reacting with the Ark, most likely," Tbilisi said.

"Is that the real Ark? Like the one in the Bible?" Bobby asked.

"Yes, it is, according to Tbilisi," Mac said.

The sun in the sky grew brighter, and when Mac looked up, he saw the moon moving toward the sun like a supernatural magnet in the sky.

"Mac, have you ever seen anything like this before?" Dante asked.

"Never, but it doesn't look good," Mac said. "The sun will eclipse, and then darkness will cover the land as Lucifer rises from Hell and takes control of this world," Tbilisi said.

"You think he knows we have the Tablet of Destinies?" Mac asked.

"He knows. He has been waiting millions of years to take this world, and if we use the Ark and tablet to set things right, he will lose his window," Tbilisi said.

"Why do you think Lucifer would have waited until now to do this?" Mac asked.

"When you broke your son out of Hell and killed one of his lieutenants, it was like spitting in the face of the devil. With the power of the Ark and her Tablet together again inside that pyramid, he will use the power to leave this dimension that is imprisoning him," Tbilisi said.

" I should have expected some repercussions, but this is ridiculous," Mac said.

"Be that as it may, we have to go now. The only ship I have that can move fast enough is our wooden pirate ride," Tbilisi said.

"What? You've got a wooden ship?" Mac asked. "Yes, it's over in the hangar at the airport. Somd of my men found it at a destroyed amusement park and brought it back here. We fitted it with a quantum drive we had found in the same place we got the trucks and guns," Tbilisi said.

"Let's go!" Ramos said.

"Yeah, the sky ain't looking too good suddenly," Dante said.

The moon stopped her race across the sky and darkened the sun until the only light reaching Earth was a dim shadow.

"That's grim, alright. Boys, I think we should do what we came here to do before we run out of time," Lilith said.

A large jeep appeared, towing a flatbed trailer. A group of Tbilisi's men tied the Ark down, securing her in place. Once the Ark was secure, Tbilisi told the driver to head to the airport. The driver nodded his head and hit the gas, knocking everyone in the back into each other.

"Can we get there in one piece?" Mac said. Jerry is a good pilot and will get us there quickly," Tbilisi said, smiling. He waved his hands in a gesture to calm down Mac.

"Sorry, it's been a long, strange trip, brother. I'm ready to see the end of it," Mac said.

"Yeah, and we're ready to return home," Dante said. Ramos and I didn't sign up for the extended stay on Earth." "I heard stories as a child that the pyramids were used as portals to other worlds or caused certain structures to act as gateways that you could walk through if you concentrated on where you wanted to go," Mac said.

"After all I've seen since we left Earth, I'm willing to believe that's at least a possibility," Bobby said. "But can the pyramids fix what I did to myself? I would never have made that mistake if I had known then what I know now."

"We'll soon see. My people were told long ago that a time would come when humanity was reborn, and another golden age of man would rise from the ashes of the old world. I never dared to believe it, but witnessing what you did for my eyes, Ramos, and the strange tales you have spoken give me faith. I believe we can turn the tide and regain our world from the evil ones," Tbilisi said.

The jeep twisted and turned down one street after another as they neared the hangar. Jerry shot through the checkpoint, flashing his badge to the guard without slowing, and raced to the hangar, where he stopped the car, and everyone got out. Tbilisi led them inside, where hovering above the floor was a giant wooden pirate ship with the name *Jolly Roger* painted on the side in haphazardly hand-drawn letters. "Nice ship," Mac said.

"Oh yes, my engineers thought it would give everyone a bit of joy to steer their pirate ship. We use it to tour the desert on occasion. The children love it," Tbilisi said.

"You've got a quantum energy drive installed in that thing? Incredible," Mac said.

"Oh yes, we'll never need gas again if we can figure out how to make more of these machines.

Now, shall we go?" Tbilisi said.

A rope ladder hung from the side, and although the ship's deck was over twenty feet above the floor, Dante had no problem leaping to the top as Serena climbed up. Mac waited until his daughter was safe aboard the ship, and then he jumped as well. Ramos followed suit and then Bobby until the only person still standing on the hangar floor was Tbilisi, and he brandished a large walking staff.

"You are all very talented," Tbilisi said. He pressed a button on the side of the staff and levitated off the floor, taking the Ark with him.

"Nice trick," Mac said, nodding.

"The staff creates a negative gravity field around me for about five feet in every direction, so whatever is in that bubble comes with me. I think the people who created this technology took it for granted," Tbilisi said. "We did trust me," Mac said.

"Who wants to drive?" Tbilisi asked.

"I do!" Dante said. "Point the way!" He was grinning from ear to ear.

Tbilisi showed Dante the controls, and within a few minutes, he was gliding out of the hanger and into the dimness of the half-sun. Although he nearly rammed the ship into a wall at first, Dante caught on quickly, and soon, they were off across the desert, sailing high above the dunes with the aid of quantum physics and twenty-first-century technology. Across the horizon, black clouds were forming close to the ground, and as they drew closer, Mac could see the great pyramid rising like a beacon, shining in the darkness of a total eclipse.

"Nice work, but how did your people repair the pyramid?" Mac asked.

"We used cone-shaped rocks that ring like a bell when struck together. They vibrate with the frequency of the Earth to levitate new blocks into place. Although it was not easy, we could also find enough granite in a hundred and fifty years to repair the outer casing stones," Tbilisi said.

"Cone-shaped rocks?" Mac asked. Tbilise Tbilisi drew the pattern in a patch of dust on the port side rail depicting what his elders used, and Mac was dumbfounded. "I don't know what to say. I'm amazed," He shook his head.

"Uh, guys. We've got company," Dante said, gripping the helm.

The Great Pyramid was within spitting distance as a volley of black-tipped arrows flew over the ship, one of them striking him directly in the chest. Dante whirled, held his hand toward the others, and took two steps forward. He was coughing and trying to get the embedded arrow out with his other hand.

"Crap! Well, this hurts like a..." Dante coughed twice more and fell over on his face.

"Dante! No!" Mac said.

He screamed in shock and anger. Below the ship, a division of angry demons swarmed in the sand, firing another volley. This one sailed over the vessel without injuring anyone, but the starboard side of the craft looked like a giant pincushion. Mac grabbed his rifle and opened fire on the demons below, picking off ten, then twenty, but more came running to battle.

"They're coming from the dark clouds!" Serena said.

Ramos walked over to his brother and turned him on his back. Knowing what he would find, Ramos steadied his mind to see that his little brother was dead. Ramos looked up into the sky and let out a long, low howl, and the warlock allowed a single tear to fall from his eye.

Dante ceased to breathe and laid still, his eyes glassy, staring into oblivion. He was at rest and no longer a part of the horror. Rage and sorrow combined to form a deadly hatred Ramos would not be able to contain for much longer as the demon within sought revenge for this travesty.

"Ramos..." Mac said.

"Save it, Mac. Just get to the pyramid and do what you have to. My brother and I are no longer a part of your conflict. I'll do what I can to stop the hordes, but my part in this tale is almost done," Ramos said.

When he looked up at Mac, there was a black tint to the purple in his eyes, as if the lights were going out and whatever sanity Ramos once had was leaving him permanently. Before Mac could utter another word, Ramos dived over the ship's side with a ferocious howl. Purple fire erupted on the battlefield as scores of demons charged Ramos. The Robe of Dragaz protected him from any magical spells as he ran forward, burning the enemy and turning them into whirlwinds of ash and soot. Mac watched as long as possible as Tbilisi took the helm and sailed the ship toward the entrance of the pyramid, a place none of the demons had reached yet. Purple flames engulfed much of the battle as Ramos let out one howl after another, his pain at the loss of his brother sending him into an abyss of insanity.

"Ramos has given us about five minutes, I imagine, but we've got to move!" Mac said.

"I'll land over there," Tbilisi said.

He docked the craft at an entrance leading down into the pyramid. Mac picked up the Ark and took Serena's backpack as he jumped overboard. When Mac landed on the ground, he felt the Ark come alive, and it began to float about two feet off the ground.

"There's a sarcophagus at the bottom of the pyramid. It would be best to place the Ark inside, open its lid, and put the tablet in. You may have to run to get out before the machine begins to generate energy. If you remain inside, you'll die," Tbilisi said. "Got it. Put the Ark in the sarcophagus, open the lid, put the tablet in, and get out. I'm all over this!"

Mac said.

He ran toward the entrance and saw a black doorway open to him. All he had to do was get inside, but suddenly, Mac was knocked off his feet by a long black tail and hit the ground with a thud.

"Dad! Watch out!" Bobby said. He was still aboard the ship when Mac fell to the ground. "Not so fast, Colonel!" The man's voice hissed inside Mac's head. "You're returning to replace my lieutenant, and then I'm burning this world to a charred husk."

"Lucifer, I presume? You've been a naughty watcher," Mac said. He was getting to his feet when he felt a jolt from behind as Lucifer sent an energy pulse into his back.

"Have some respect, fool!" Lucifer said.

Mac rose again but was knocked to the ground with so much force that he began to bleed inside his chest. Coughing out the crimson liquid, he started to feel helpless for the first time in a long time.

Serena was still on the ship with Tbilisi when Bobby snuck away and jumped off the other side. He crept around behind Lucifer and his father, unnoticed by the devil. Bobby used his good fortune to grab the levitating Ark and tablet and dived inside the pyramid a split second before Lucifer looked his way. He focused his attention on Mac and failed to see that the Ark and the tablet were no longer lying on the ground. Bobby ran inside, his mind racing a thousand miles an hour, desperate to get the Ark where it needed to be before it was too late. Down he went into some of the tightest spaces he had ever seen, but once inside, he felt a strange power, as if there was an aura to the ancient structure. "Are you alive?" Bobby asked as he ran.

Finally, he found the carved stone box and placed the Ark inside, feeling the power inside the artifact corrupting his physical makeup. He watched the Ark awaken as small bolts of electricity passed between the angels with outstretched arms. With fear in his heart, he opened the lid to place the tablet inside. The Ark was filled with a powdery white substance, and as he introduced the tablet, the white turned to blue. Bobby dropped the lid and ran the way he had come in.

The Ark was now an electrical transformer, and the combined power of the Ark, tablet, and pyramid caused a funnel of white-hot energy to shoot through the top of the structure and exit through a prismatic crystal sitting atop the ancient structure. Bobby was almost at the exit when the power from within blew him forward, tossing his body into the air like a ragdoll, and he was spat out of the pyramid with the force of a bullet from a rifle. Lucifer saw the energy discharge and stopped his attack on Mac.

"What have you done to me?!" Lucifer screamed. Smoke rose from his skin, and he began to smolder. He was furious and enraged but impotent against the power of light shining forth. Lucifer and his followers vanished with a loud crack. The moon began to move back to its former position in the sky, releasing the sun's rays to abolish Lucifer's presence on the Earthly plane.

Light from the pyramid split in every direction, casting its divine energy upon all as it traveled to all of the ancient megalithic pyramidal structures, reinvigorating them, charging their crystals and stones with positive energy as the Earth renewed herself once more. The demons were turned to ash, and all of the portals generated by the Tesla towers closed forever. The rusted hulks, once thought to be the last hope for humanity, collapsed in rusted heaps and were never used again. Mac ran over to Bobby, who was picking himself up as Serena joined them, and then Lilith.

"Kids, look!" Mac said.

Trees bloomed in the desert, and up from the ground, a river of fresh water rose from the center of the Earth. Bushes took root, and grass grew where life had been nonexistent for thousands of years.

"The Earth is repairing herself. Praise be to God!" Tbilisi said.

"All the hard work and heavy lifting were worth it, Dad!" Bobby said.

"Bobby, look at your arms!" Mac said. Pink human skin was bubbling to the surface of his forearms, and Bobby was reverting to his human form once more. The curse had been broken at the dawn of the fifth age of man.

Lilith landed and walked over to stand next to Mac and his children.

Tbilisi walked over next to the small family and smiled, bowing his head to them.

"My friends, our entire planet is indebted to you and your bravery. Your story will be told, and songs sung about you all," Tbilisi said.

Having survived the battle, Ramos sauntered toward them, his robe tattered, exhaustion written on his face. Part of his left ear was torn, and his fur was wet with blood patches.

"Ramos!" Serena said. She screeched and ran at him, embracing the warlock with all her might.

"You made it, buddy!" Mac said.

"Yes, and now I believe it is time to leave. Does anyone have an idea how I can do that? I need to take my brother home and mourn my loss," Ramos said.

Everyone looked to Tbilisi, who nodded his head. "Now that balance has been restored to this world, the chants in my family book of spells should work to get you home, Ramos. You will need to have unbroken concentration and think of nothing but home and where you want to go while I perform the spell." "Hey, what did I miss?" Dante said. His voice was weak as he leaned over the side of the ship, the arrow in his hand.

Ramos' eyes widened. Then he smiled, and his eyes flashed a vibrant violet.

"Dante! You old son of a gun! Welcome back," Mac said.

"I was floating above my body, watching all of you in slow motion, when I saw a flash of light and boom! I was back," Dante said.

Tbilisi drew a circle in the dirt with his staff and took a small book from his pocket. He began to recite lyrics from the small book, and as he spoke, the dirt circle formed a green pool of light. Ramos closed his eyes and concentrated on him until he could see Wasatch Woods in his mind. Then, as the pool whirled in a clockwise circle, it cleared, and all watching could see Stephanie and Kim standing in the village chatting with a group of wolven women. The circle rose from the ground, forming a large doorway between worlds. The two human women looked up astonished as Mac waved for them to jump through. Stephanie grabbed her daughter like a football, and without a second thought, they ran for the door and jumped from one world to the next. "You guys are a sight for sore eyes! We thought we'd never get home," Stephanie said. She started to cry, and so did Kim.

Dante jumped down from the *Jolly Roger* and joined Ramos by the doorway, still holding his wounded side.

"We've got to go, Mac. You know, you're welcome to join us," Ramos said.

"Yeah, there's still a lot of Eritria we haven't shown you," Dante said.

Mac looked at Tbilisi with a curious grin, and the old man returned it.

"You have done more than enough for the planet, Colonel MacDonald. We are the caretakers of this world now. Go, find another adventure, spread the word to other worlds the miracle that has happened here," Tbilisi said.

Mac looked over at Lilith, she cocked her head and smiled. "What do you want to do?"

"Kids?" Mac asked.

"We're with you until the end, Dad," Bobby said. "Yeah," Serena said.

Mac looked at Stephanie and Kim, who each gave him an uncomfortable glance.

"Neither of you are required to do anything more than you already have," Mac said. "I'm staying here, Mac," Stephanie said. "I want to raise my daughter here on Earth."

"I want to stay as well," Kim said.

"You have to do what's best for yourselves. Our war is over, and your service to the country would have been satisfied over one hundred and fifty years ago. If that country still existed, that is."

Mac gave each of them a hug.

"Thank you for your service to the planet and our mission. You're both heroes," Mac said.

Ramos and Dante stepped through the portal, followed by the children, and then Mac and Lilith stepped across. Mac turned around one final time to see Tbilisi smiling, a hand raised in a farewell gesture, and then the portal between Earth and Eritria vanished.

www.ingramcontent.com/pod-product-compliance
Lightning Source LLC
Chambersburg PA
CBHW070926260626
47162CB00007B/2803